A New God in Town

Book 2
of the Red State/Blue State Confessions

Thomas Keech

Real
Nice Books
Baltimore, Maryland

ISBN 978-1-7330524-6-7 Hardback
ISBN 978-1-7330524-7-4 Paperback
ISBN 978-1-7330524-8-1 Ebook

Library of Congress Control Number
2020936609

Published by

Real
Nice Books
11 Dutton Court, Suite 606
Baltimore, Maryland 21228
www.realnicebooks.com

Publisher's note: This is a work of fiction. Names, characters, places, institutions, and incidents are entirely the product of the author's imagination or are used fictitiously, and any resemblance to actual persons, living or dead, or to events, incidents, institutions, or places is entirely coincidental.

Cover photo by Shutterstock/Dark Room Pictures
Set in Sabon.

The Confessions

~

The Red State/Blue State Confessions is a dystopian series set in the very near future in Kansas and Massachusetts. The United States has essentially split into two different countries. Stacey Davenport fights back against a regime that is quickly reducing women to concubinage in Kansas.

Even as a motorcycle gang, deputized as religious police, rounds up the designated women, Stacey starts a political campaign to overthrow the regime. But Stacey's initial victory does not really change the status quo on the ground in certain parts of Kansas. Now, while Stacey fights in Topeka for the legal right to keep her unborn baby girl, her sister must risk her life in a daring rescue attempt.

For Rea

Chapter 1

Amy stepped carefully around the charred ruins of her family home. Her mother's old truck was still there in the back, peppered with soot, the green paint on the passenger side door now singed a dark brown. But it looked like it might still run. The family had split up since the Genesis Riders had burned down the house, and nobody seemed to be thinking much about the truck. Good.

Over the past year, Amy had taken the truck out a few times without her mother's permission – secretly, of course, because she was fifteen and didn't have a license. And now that she was branded, she would never be able to drive legally. That was why this particular truck was so critical to their plan. Because it was registered in her mother's name, it could go anywhere without much chance of being tracked. Conception Control usually didn't bother tracking the vehicles of females over forty.

A rustling in the weeds behind startled her. She turned around, ready to run; but then she saw Ruth approaching from the other side of the ruined house.

"Does it run?" Ruth asked as she came near, murmuring her words as if she feared someone might overhear, even though they were on the outskirts of Cosgrove, Kansas, and there wasn't another human in sight. Amy knew this degree of caution was ridiculous here, in this safe county. But she hadn't suffered as much as Ruth had at the hands of the Riders.

Ruth was nineteen, tall, slim, broad-shouldered, with the naturally erect posture of a model, or a soldier. She wore her red hair in a rough approximation of a pixie cut. She attracted attention in the streets of Cosgrove even before she started carrying the nine-millimeter Glock. Her lips were full but usually set in a determined line. She was the only woman who had ever escaped captivity in Neola County. When she spoke of her disdain for the Genesis Riders or Reverend Ezekial, her green eyes glowed with the commitment of a convert.

"Let's get in the truck." Ruth still talked as if someone were eavesdropping on them. "Does it have any gas?" Ruth had grown up in Neola County, on her father's farm. Her father was a zealous follower of the Reverend Ezekial. He listened daily to Ezekial's podcasts and followed religiously the minister's detailed instructions for family life. Following those directives, her father had refused to allow her to get a driver's license, to drive the tractor on the farm, or to operate any type of machinery at all. The only exception was the family sewing machine. As a result, all Ruth knew about trucks was that they needed gas. Amy was going to have to be the driver.

They had decided the safest plan was to take off right away if the truck started. They would leave the civilized confines of Cosgrove County and search for Ruth's sister in Neola County. If they were caught in Neola County, they would almost certainly be taken captive and disappear into the concubine underground. But still, as Ruth had explained to Amy, they couldn't wait forever. Renee was already three months pregnant. Once Renee's baby was born, her owner could do whatever he wanted with the child.

Amy was not only providing the truck; she was also providing the only viable plan for finding Renee. Every woman taken in Neola County was assigned to be the second or third wife to a man chosen by the clergy, that is to say by Reverend Ezekial. The assignments were secret. The addresses of the concubines were not given out. The Genesis Riders brutalized any family members who demanded answers. The system was illegal, but Ezekial had such a political stranglehold on the county, and the Genesis Riders such control of the streets, that the sheriff went out of his way to look the other way.

Their entire rescue plan was based on their faith in Don, Amy's father. It was Don who had rescued Ruth from her chains within a day of her being taken captive. It was Don who took her to the hospital for the burns on her legs, then took her to the women's shelter in Cosgrove, then took her to the family house, where Amy's mother took her in. Ruth had met Amy there, and they had become friends.

The rescue had been a one-off, a lucky break for Ruth, who had been in the right place at the right time. But Ruth's faith in Don was unwavering. Amy's faith in her father was coming back. Don was the only person in the resistance who could travel freely in Neola County without being tracked. He was probably the only person who could help them find Renee. They needed to find him first. Amy prayed that he hadn't been captured.

*** ***

Amy drove fast enough to get to her father's old hideout 25 miles away in in Neola before they were in too much danger of being tracked, but slow enough not to be stopped for speeding. No one cared about the actual speed limit on the dead straight roads between flat fields of drying cornstalks and sorghum, so she settled on 85. The wide sky was a gloomy grey from horizon to horizon, but there was no rain yet. Amy told Ruth she had driven this route numerous times to deliver food to her father. This was back when food was the only thing he could be trusted with. Later, during the election campaign, they'd used his hideaway as a way station for women fleeing the Genesis Riders.

They pulled the truck behind a lonely white clapboard building that was close to the road and bordered by overgrowths of scrub trees and honeysuckle. The slowly deteriorating building had over the years housed a number of different small businesses, and it now served as a vinyl record store with a couple of tiny apartments in the back. A few other decrepit buildings haunted that stretch of road, but none of the others was occupied. A gravel driveway circled behind the record store and then back out to the road. Amy pulled the truck quietly to a stop in back. A weathered wooden staircase led to a second-story back porch, off of which there were the two apartments. Amy's father, Don, had lived there for months trying to escape the brutality being inflicted on addicts in Neola County.

"Why is there crime scene tape on the steps?" Ruth asked quietly.

"Two markos were shot here a few weeks ago." The new laws required the branding of felons and addicts. Markos were people who had been branded.

"Who did it?"

"Probably the Genesis Riders. Stacey and my brother Kendrick were out here at the time. I think they saw it happen."

"What did they see?"

"I don't know."

"What do you mean? What did they say happened?"

"They won't say anything about it." Amy turned to Ruth. "You gotta understand my family. Like, keeping secrets from one another, that's normal for us."

The cab of the pickup was hot even in the shade from the scrub trees. They decided they would go up the stairs together. Each ancient board creaked as they stepped on it. Ruth kept her hand on the butt of her gun. They knocked on the door of Don's hideaway apartment first and got no answer. They knocked on the other apartment door. No response. They went back to the truck and waited. "He's got no phone, no device, no GPS. No address. Nothing. There's no way to find him but to wait here."

Ruth nodded. They hadn't expected this to be easy.

They waited at least an hour. The sky darkened and a misty rain began to fall. They kept the windows cracked so the windshield wouldn't completely fog up. The cab filled up with a damp odor of perspiration and soap.

"You don't know for sure if he lives here?" Ruth was getting edgy.

"He did live here. He can't go back to his old rehab center in this county even if he wanted to, because it burned down. He has another place where he makes things, an old machine shop or something, but I don't know where it is. I don't think he sleeps there anyway. We have to wait to see if he comes back. It's our only chance."

"The longer we're out here, the bigger the risk."

The thousands of tiny raindrops on the driver's side window suddenly flashed like beads of lightning. There was a loud rap on the glass.

*** ***

Amy jumped, then caught her breath and looked over at Ruth. Ruth reached for her gun.

"Are you two okay?" A muffled voice could be heard from the other side of the glass.

Amy rolled down the window. The two girls exhaled together in relief. This could be worse, Amy told herself. Whoever this was, he was not a Genesis Rider, and he was not even on a motorcycle. She saw a skinny young guy with blonde hair, fairly tall, holding a flashlight with one hand and a yellow poncho over his head with the other.

"Um, yes, we're okay."

The flashlight played around the cab, resting for a moment on Ruth's gun. Amy calculated how long it would take to turn the key in the ignition, put the truck in gear and peel out of there. The beam followed from the gun to Ruth's wrists to her arms to her shoulders to her neck. If he shone the light right in Ruth's eyes, Amy decided, she would start the truck and pull out of there even if she had to drag the guy halfway back to Cosgrove. But the beam retreated and shone on Amy. Amy shook her hair to make sure her bangs covered up the brand on her forehead.

"Oh, I know you. You're the girl who used to drive up here every week. I thought I recognized your truck."

"I don't know who you are."

"Damien. I work in the record store. You used to bring food to that marko. That marko, he's your father or something, right?"

"Damien," she said. Amy felt like she gained a little control by using his name. "Do you know where my father is now?"

"No." The flashlight beam played over both of them again.

"Damien, have you called anybody? Have you told anybody that you saw us here tonight?"

"Why is she carrying a gun?"

Amy turned the key and started the engine. But he leaned in further. Water dripped from his plastic poncho onto her arm. Ruth gripped the gun in both hands. Taking off would be too risky for everybody. Amy took her foot off the gas.

Amy's words just poured out. "We're searching for my father. We're in danger if we stay here too long. Please let us go."

The motor was still running. He was still leaning in. Water was still dripping on Amy's arm. Ruth's gun was now pointing straight ahead at the dash. Amy realized that Ruth saw only two options, run or shoot. She had to hope there were more.

Chapter 2

Stacey Davenport had arrived at the legislature in Topeka without a single legislative ally. There were very few people in the statehouse who would even look her in the eye. Not that everybody in the statehouse, and most of the people in Kansas, didn't know her name. Her tumultuous election campaign and its violent aftermath had been covered in the national news. Public opinion of her was about equally split. They either loved her or hated her. But even among the legislators who shared her beliefs, there was nobody who had the courage to step forward and welcome her on that first day.

Reverend Ezekial's Certainty Party still had complete control over the legislature. They continued to pass bills placing the government in more and more control over women's lives. Governor Adams was not in the Certainty Party, but she had reluctantly signed most of these bills in her first year in office. But she drew the line at MOMS. The Make Our Motherhood Strong Act, or MOMS as it was popularly called, would require all unmarried women with children, and all unmarried women who were pregnant, and all of their sisters over the age of twelve, to be removed from their homes and assigned by the clergy as second or third wives to a married parishioner for proper training and discipline, and a life of service.

Governor Adams vetoed the bill. The burning question in Stacey's campaign had been whether the legislature would override the veto and make MOMS the law of the state. The Kansas Senate easily overrode the veto, casting several votes more than the two-thirds necessary. The vote in the House would be closer. Stacey's entire reason for running for office had been to make sure MOMS didn't get its two-thirds majority in the House. The vote was taken on the House floor on the day she first arrived in the legislature.

The Speaker of the House raised the stakes by calling for a roll call vote on the House floor. The local media was controlled almost entirely by billionaire Robert Golsch, and there was no doubt the names of all the heretics who voted against God's will would be trumpeted throughout Kansas. The delegates were called in alphabetical order. But Stacey noticed the Speaker skipped over her name. The votes in favor of overriding the veto and enacting MOMS climbed steadily. There were 82 votes for MOMS. Everybody but Stacey had voted. MOMS needed one more vote to overcome the governor's veto.

The Speaker pretended to be confused. "Oh, I left out one name. Our new delegate. Delegate Davenporn." The mispronunciation was deliberate. "Delegate Davenporn, how do you vote, in favor of God or against Him?"

"Davenport. I vote *no*. I vote *not* to override the veto." She went on, even though giving a speech at this point was out of order. "MOMS has finally been defeated, thanks to the bravery of thousands of women across this state."

"Delegate Davenporn, may I remind you of the Word of God as set out in the New Testament: *A woman should learn in quietness and full submission*. Full submission. Do you persist in defying God's Word with your vote?"

"My vote is still no."

Stacey was assigned the worst office suite in the state house, down in the basement. The short, rectangular windows were up near the ceiling and provided only a dim light and a view of the shoes of passers-by. Stacey's mother, Audrey, had insisted they have a little celebration of the vote there. Stacey's status as a recovering addict had prepared her well for the bland, non-alcoholic reception that took place in her legislative office suite. Audrey and Stacey's younger brother were mingling and making small talk, trying to break the ice with the few Independent Party members who dared to come. People were standing around, drinking white grape juice from clear cups. She wished her father could be there. Don had helped in her campaign more than anyone else would ever know. He had saved her life. But then he had disappeared on election night.

A few delegates across the room toasted her with upraised plastic glasses, but nobody approached her. Clearly, nobody knew what to think. People around her during her campaign had died. She had carried on a notorious affair with a married man. She had publicly agreed at one point to become a concubine herself. No one came up to her now.

"Honey, you're a politician now. You've got to talk to people." The events of the campaign had brought out Audrey's organizational and people skills. For the first time in years, Stacey's mother was giving good advice to her daughter rather than whining about her own domestic situation. Still, Stacey didn't think of herself as a politician. She wasn't going to go up to the other delegates and drink grape juice and talk about the weather. But some of the Independents were the very people who had held out against MOMS. She owed them. She knew she should thank them. And there was a lot more work they all needed do together.

Stacey was glad to hear a name she was familiar with. Martha Smarks was one of the leading Independents. The Independents had been the only group consistently on the side of women's freedom. The Democrats and Republicans had wished and washed all over the issue. These traditional parties were very much under the sway of Robert Golsch, a multi-billionaire oligarch who controlled a big part of the business and agriculture sector, not to mention almost all of the media, in Kansas. In the last year, Golsch seemed to have formed an unholy alliance with Reverend Ezekial's Certainty Party. In return for the Certainty Party's total support for his business agenda, Golsch had gone along with their schemes to control women's bodies, their domestic relations, their access to the professions, their freedom of movement. Golsch then put the pressure on the Democrats and Republicans to go along too. Both parties totally caved. All the bills restricting women's rights had been successful until Stacey and the Independents mustered the votes necessary to defeat MOMS.

"Martha, I'm glad to meet you." Stacey put out her hand. She was relieved that Martha shook it. That was a start. Martha was about five four, a few inches shorter than Stacey, and she couldn't have been a more different physical type. While Stacey had dark eyes and long chestnut hair, Martha had blonde hair, a long face, and a serious blue-eyed stare. She looked ultra-thin and healthy and businesslike in her light blue wool suit. Stacey had admired the ease with which she chatted up even Stacey's mother and brother.

"Congratulations on your hard-fought victory, Stacey. It couldn't be more consequential. You have literally saved thousands of women in this state from servitude."

"I'm just one vote. You Independents have been the ones holding off Reverend Ezekial from turning Kansas into a total hell on earth for women. But thanks. It's a good day, isn't it?"

But Martha wanted to talk about the downside. "But at what a terrible cost to you! And to us! You can't believe what a blow Roland's death was to the Independents. He was our leader. So charismatic." Martha was talking and breathing fast. It wasn't the grape juice. "Stacey, I can see how anybody would want to become ... um ... *involved* with him. I know you must have horribly mixed feelings today. So, I .... Besides congratulating you, I also want to sympathize with you for your loss."

Stacey wondered if she should just tell her the truth. She had thought she was in love with Roland. But the relationship had started off wrong and quickly went from bad to worse. The grisly end to it had been plastered all over the media.

Half the country blamed her for Roland's death.

Stacey was not sure she would ever publicly share the full story of her political and sexual union with Roland. There were other people involved who could still be hurt. She tried to turn the conversation to efforts to get some of last year's misogynous laws repealed.

But Martha clearly didn't want to let go of the conversation about Roland. "In the church, after your little brother stood up and objected to your marriage, you said you loved Roland despite everything and were proud to become his second wife." Martha had seen the news videos, as had practically everyone else in Kansas. "I'm just saying, I know he was forcing you to say that. But there must have been some truth in what you said. I don't know ...."

Martha's voice trailed off as Stacey studied her face. Was Martha trying to decide, like most other people in Topeka, whether to treat Stacey like a self-sacrificing saint, a woman who had been out of her depth in love, or a scheming political whore? But she didn't seem to be studying Stacey at all. Her blue eyes widened and seemed to focus on something only she could see. And she didn't seem to want to let go of the conversation about Roland.

"No woman should ever be the property of a man – and that's what MOMS would have done." Stacey knew she was preaching, but she felt more comfortable preaching than in revealing all the strands of love and despair that made up her personal life. She hoped Martha would stay on safe political grounds, too. "We beat down MOMS. Now we've got to try to walk back the other anti-women laws."

But Martha persisted, her eyes wide and seemingly lost in some sorrow of her own. "I mean, I miss him. He was our guiding light. I've never had a friend so intelligent, and kind, and wise. I really, really miss him."

*** ***

Stacey's family had been forced to split up when their house was burned down on election night. Stacey had decided to stay in the apartment Roland had rented for them. It wasn't like she was living in Roland's actual former home. It was a sparsely-furnished place, technically his legislative office. They had used it as their bedroom so as to keep their distance from his wife, Frieda. It was close to the legislature in Topeka. She wasn't even sure how much the rent was. But when she went to the rental office to try to find out, the people there told her the rent had been paid in advance for a year. She was surprised Roland had paid so far ahead. She didn't have any source of income other than her paltry legislative salary, so she decided to stay in the apartment until someone told her to leave.

Ever since her election, she had been waiting for the axe to fall: for Frieda, or Roland's estate, or someone from Roland's family to call and tell her to get out, but it hadn't happened. She still had to spend some time in her mother's rented house in Cosgrove also, because she was the town's representative, and she needed to officially reside there. But she spent most of her nights in the virtually empty apartment in Topeka.

Even as the women of her Cosgrove district flocked to her as their savior, and even as the Independents in Topeka began to respect her, she felt more and more degraded on a personal level. She was starting to appreciate the underside of her affair with Roland. She had genuinely admired him. But she now felt guilty for having so smoothly and easily cast aside her morals and gone after the husband of another woman, a woman who had been her friend. And when Roland had dangled in front of her the expectation of becoming the political savior of all the women in Kansas, she had totally compromised herself for that goal. She had killed off her heart for a political objective, and her personal life now seemed as seedy and debased as it had been during her drug-driven teenage years.

She was lonely, and she had to fight back every day against the feeling that she deserved to be alone. She realized it was probably just a daydream that her former boyfriend, Grant, would want to be involved with her any more. Over the past few weeks, she had begun to blame herself for their breakup. If, three months ago, she had answered any of his calls or texts or tweets and forgiven him for his moment of panic, she never would have gotten involved with Roland. Marriage to Grant would have been messy, with her legally confined to Kansas due to Conception Control and Grant tied to his high-tech company in Boston. But he was a good man who really had loved her. She had panicked as much as he had. Now she faced the prospect of raising her child alone, creating yet another generation of the broken Davenport family.

Chapter 3

The water from Damien's poncho was still dripping onto Amy's legs. He wasn't being aggressive, but it seemed he would not go away. Amy saw Ruth tighten her hold on the gun.

"Damien, would you please help us?" Amy suddenly implored. "We can't afford to be caught out here alone by the Genesis Riders."

"Sure. But I haven't seen your father." The rain kept spattering the windshield, and his poncho. "Nobody's been up in that apartment for a couple of weeks."

"Are you all alone in that store?"

"Yeah. Nobody comes in after 3:00. Nobody comes if it rains."

"Do you think we could come in for a minute, at least? We really need to use the rest room."

He dipped his head further into the window, dripping more on Amy, but looking at Ruth. "Sure. But can she put that gun down first?"

Amy had expected the store to sell only dusty thirty-year-old records in moldy cardboard jackets, but most of the stock was new. The wooden bins the albums were stacked in, however, looked like they were at least fifty years old. Damien seemed a lot more comfortable with the two of them once Ruth's gun was safely tucked away. He told them vinyl was the newest thing. He said it sounded better, and you didn't have to listen to ads or be assaulted by pop-ups. He obviously believed this choice of music formats really mattered.

He showed them the rest room at the end of a long, creaking wooden corridor. It was an ancient bathroom left over from one of the building's previous uses. When Amy came back from using it, she noticed that Damien and Ruth weren't speaking, or even making eye contact. Amy understood that Ruth was not a chatty person, but Damien seemed the opposite. The two of them were hardly being civil. Maybe it was the gun.

"What do you do here all day, all by yourself?" Amy started.

Damien was standing behind the counter. The stiffness in his stance melted away as soon as Amy began talking to him. "Listen to music. Connect with my friends." He seemed like he was waiting for Amy to ask another question. When she didn't, he went on and explained himself anyway. "I have another business, too. A security alarm and camera business."

"Oh, that's cool," Amy encouraged him. "It's your own business?"

"Yeah." He smiled. "It's very small right now. When nobody's in here – which is most of the time – I design systems and put them together in here. Deliver and install on my own time." He moved his hands when he talked as if he were displaying the devices to Amy. It was obvious he was energized by being the center of her undivided attention.

"Cool," Amy responded.

"What about you?" he asked.

"I'm just in high school."

"What about you?" He turned to Ruth, who seemed startled that he would talk to her.

Ruth stayed back near the wall but made sure she was heard. "I'm a former captive of the Genesis Riders. They burned my legs. They took me to Reverend Ezekial, who chained me in his backyard cabana. Don, Amy's father – the guy we're looking for – he's the one who rescued me." She stared at him. "We need to find him. Is that enough information?"

"Oh." Damien grimaced. His face went a whiter shade of pale. He turned around without responding to Ruth, picked out a few albums and gazed blankly at the album notes like he had forgotten the two women were there. He seemed to be waiting for them to go. Eventually he turned back and faced them, leaning forward, his hands flat on the counter, his weight on his hands. "Okay. You need to find him. I understand." He shook his head vaguely. "I didn't know the Genesis Riders were that bad." He returned their stares, defensive now. "I've never seen anything about this on the news, or online."

"Ezekial and his friends control all the news in this county," Ruth informed him. "Everybody's postings are under surveillance. Anybody who posts anything negative is likely to get hurt. You've been sitting in this dead-end record store for too long." Ruth was nothing if not blunt.

Amy tried for a softer note. "That's why we had to come here in person, with no electronics. And we can't stay long. But, do you think you could possibly kind of look out for my father?"

"… and call you if he comes back? Sure, I'll just text you."

"Don't do that. Conception Control monitors all communications of all females over the age of twelve. You don't want to get us in trouble with them. Maybe you can text my brother, maybe use some kind of code."

"Sure." Damien's eyes met Amy's. "I'm good with codes. Give me your brother's number." She did, and they leaned together over the counter and figured out a simple code. "Put it in your phone."

"I can't carry a phone in this county. Just write it down."

He wrote it on the back of a sales slip and slid it across the counter to her. Amy met his eyes again. "Do you promise you'll let us know the minute you see my father around here?"

"Sure. But Amy, I might be able to do better than that. The Genesis Riders come in here sometimes. I hear them talk about what they're up to. I'll let you know anything I hear."

Chapter 4

If Stacey had learned anything from her many humiliating experiences of the past few months, it was that when things went wrong, there was usually plenty of blame to go around. Grant was the father of her unborn child. True, he hadn't reacted to the announcement as she had hoped. But she was the one who had blocked out all further communications from Grant. She was the one who took up with Roland soon afterwards. She was the one who obeyed Roland's every sick command until she was humiliated in front of the entire state.

The breakup with Grant had come about two months earlier. He had shocked her by literally running out of his apartment in Boston the minute she first told him she was pregnant. It had seemed a brutal end to the deep love she had thought they shared. Once she got back on the plane to Kansas, there was no going back. Under the Conception Control laws, she would not be able to leave Kansas again until after the baby was born. She had felt there was no sense answering his calls or texts after that. She had totally ghosted him.

But then he had shocked her by coming to Kansas, uninvited, in the middle of her campaign, seemingly unafraid of the threats of violence against her and all her supporters. His company even helped finance her campaign. But Grant never did consent to becoming Stacey's friend again. He said he would be her political ally, and nothing more. In the chaos of election night, he had been competent and kind, but he left soon afterwards. He had once said he wanted to be involved with their child when it was born, but she hadn't heard from him since he left. She hadn't realized how much his absence would continue to hurt.

But she knew she had better things to do now than chase after Grant. She knew she had to find allies in the legislature. Most of the men there were hesitant to talk with her. They surely recognized her as a new political force, but they seemed hesitant to make the usual political overtures. She understood. Her checkered personal history could endanger the reputation of any male politician who might be seen working closely with her. The mystery surrounding Roland's death seemed to frighten them into silence. She wasn't going to make real friends among the male politicians. She had learned to accept that. She had to own what she had done. Once upon a time, Grant had helped her believe in herself, but she would have to find that belief on her own now.

Chapter 5

One of the first things Grant had to do when he arrived back in Boston was to hire a new legal assistant for the office. On his first morning back, Grant and Amos, the owner of the company, interviewed the very first applicant for the job, a second-year law student named Eleni. Eleni admitted she had little experience in commercial or patent law, but she seemed intelligent, and mature for her age. Beautiful, with penetrating brown eyes and dark hair curved under in a silky bob, she was almost painfully direct. She was just 23 but seemed to have the grace and gravity of a much older woman. At her interview, she focused only on the job duties, the working conditions, her qualifications, and what she could learn from the job. She apologized that she'd have to be gone most weeknights to attend law classes. She said she had no intention of asking the company to comply with the new state law that required them to give her 15 hours a week paid time to study. She told Grant and Amos that she knew that a lawyer in a start-up company might be asked to research any kind of law, any time of day or night. She seemed so interested and competent that Amos consulted in private with Grant for ten minutes, then hired her on the spot.

When she reported for work the first day, Grant realized that the confidence she displayed in the interview had been a little bit of an act. She blanched when he showed her a demand letter from a national software company that Liotech cease and desist from using its code – and then ordered her to draft a reply.

"Honestly, I don't know anything about software, or coding," she confessed.

"Neither do I. Your job is to figure it out."

She disappeared into the tiny office right next door to his

for a week, coming out only to talk to the Liotech software developers from time to time. When she came back to Grant's office, she had an opinion.

"I think what our company is doing is okay," she ventured. "But you really should go over what I've been looking at. This is all new to me."

"I don't have time."

"Oh … then …." He could see why she had stopped in mid-sentence. She wouldn't, couldn't admit any fear. But he could see it in her eyes.

"It's okay," he relented. "I'll find time to look at it." The relief in her eyes was so obvious he had to smile. "Don't worry. It gets easier. I'll try to help you when I have time."

That first assignment had been sort of a test. Her other assignments were usually easier, sometimes just cite-checking his briefs and pleadings. She did this very well. In a few instances she updated his research with more recent cases he hadn't noticed. This was her first real job since she graduated from college.

She seemed not only pleasant and cooperative with the other workers, but she also had a fair knowledge of the latest Massachusetts Rules of Ethno-Civility. She followed those workplace laws religiously – and was the first employee who had ever done so with such apparent ease. Because there was some danger that she and Grant were too ethno-similar, she had volunteered to take a DNA test. Because there was enough contrast between her predominantly Mediterranean ancestry and Grant's Irish and Spanish background, she was hired, though Jeanine Atwood, the office manager, said it was a close call. She said the next hire probably couldn't be from that DNA sector at all. Grant breathed a sigh of relief.

But after a few weeks, word got around the office that she didn't think Grant liked her. He was puzzled about this. He called her in to talk about that. "That's not true at all. I think you're doing very well. We do need another lawyer still, but I think you're doing well as our legal assistant."

Eleni hunched her shoulders as if she were waiting for the other shoe to drop. "But … what?" she stammered.

"But nothing. You're doing fine. We all like you."

She still seemed uncomfortable. Grant was puzzled. His instinct was to comfort her. She was eager and beautiful and worried, the picture of the classic damsel in distress. He knew he had to hold himself back, but he couldn't completely stop himself.

"Is there something I'm doing that makes you think that I'm disappointed in you?"

"No. It's just, just …." She gradually raised her eyes to him, her posture no longer that of the shrinking damsel. "You've have consistently said I'm doing okay. I appreciate that. This is my first real professional job. I'm learning what to expect … *and what not to expect*." He looked at her quizzically. She went on, her tone now more businesslike. "You have been everything to me a good supervisor should be. And I'm happy with that. And I'm glad to be here."

As quietly as he could, Grant asked around about her in the next few days. People reported a change in Eleni; they said seemed happier on the job now. He wondered what all the fuss had been about. He also wondered what it was that Eleni had learned *not* to expect.

"What is it?" he asked Amos. "What is it that she had to learn *not* to expect? Did she think we were going to hire her full time, as a lawyer or something, right off the bat?"

"You can't figure this out?" Amos looked at him incredulously. "She's beautiful. She expected special treatment. Or at least to be hit on."

"That doesn't happen in Massachusetts."

"You are so naïve, Grant."

That wasn't the last personnel problem concerning Eleni's

employment. The issue of her ethnic ancestry came up again, this time by a twist in the law that caught Grant by surprise. Although DNA was the most accurate and scientific way to determine one's ethnicity, there was a blue-state movement of people who refused to give their DNA for analysis. Their primary demand was to let each person determine his or her own racial/ethnic makeup. It wasn't hard to see how easily this system would be to manipulate, and what a monkey wrench this would throw into a system based on racial/ethnic quotas. The various blue states struggled with these demands in various ways. The Massachusetts legislature simply closed its eyes and declared that both methods of determining one's racial or ethnic identity were valid. Each citizen was given the absolute right to determine his or her ethnic identity by either DNA or free choice. Whatever choice each citizen made would be factored into the mandatory quotas for schooling, government housing, government jobs, or private hiring. Each citizen could also change his or her ethnic identity, though not more often than once a year.

None of this had much effect on Grant's life until Jeanine Atwood, the office manager, decided suddenly to change her ethnicity from German-American to Italian. As Jeanine well knew, this created an imbalance, with an excess of Mediterranean heritage. Someone had to go. Eleni was the last hire with Mediterranean heritage, and she was told they would have to let her go.

Grant was upset. He asked to see Jeanine in her office.

"Why are you doing this?"

"I don't have to tell you. No one has to explain to their employer why they changed their identity."

"I'm not your employer. I'm just a co-worker. We all get along so well here. People seem to like Eleni. Why are you trying to get rid of her?"

"I'm doing this for your own good, Grant."

"What do you mean?"

"It's obvious she's in love with you, Grant."

"What! Oh, come on."

"I've been a personnel manager for a long time. Nothing good can come of that. We'll give her a great reference. She deserves it. She'll do fine."

His anger drove him to his feet. "You're not serious. I'm not interested in her. And even if I did want to get personally involved with Eleni, we could file a PR-26 Form. You of all people should know it's legal to have a personal relationship with someone at work, as long as you file the form and follow all the PR-26 procedures."

"I'm doing it for your own good. And hers. The poor girl's suffering."

"I don't believe this!" He stormed out of the office and ran to find Amos. Amos and Grant had become friends in the year they had worked together getting the company to prosper. But Amos didn't seem too concerned about this problem until Grant threatened to quit.

"Hold on. Calm down, Grant. Why don't you just change your own identity? You could be anything: Ethiopian, Arab, Chinese."

"Because ... because ... I don't know why. Yes, I do. Stupid reason, I guess. Because my parents would be disappointed in me."

"They'll never know."

"I'm not doing it, Amos. That's the bottom line. I'm not even interested in Eleni. It's just wrong, what Jeanine's doing. You've got to stand up for your employees."

Employers were not supposed to try to influence their employees' choices of identity. Nevertheless, Jeanine changed her mind, supposedly on her own. Shortly afterwards, she was given a $20,000 bonus.

As he had hoped, Eleni didn't say thank you, didn't act

any differently toward him; if anything, she acted even more formal toward him. He felt he had acted decisively, and for the good.

He couldn't understand how Jeanine had gotten the idea that he and Eleni were starting a personal relationship. Not an inappropriate word, gesture or look had ever passed between them. He was going to have a child by another woman in another state, and the thought of messing around with Eleni had never crossed his mind. Of course, the other-woman-in-another-state business hadn't worked out well. He had even chased after Stacey with the secret hope of patching things up, but that hadn't worked out at all. He had just made things worse.

Chapter 6

Roland's burial was in the beautiful Mount Hope Cemetery in Topeka. Roland's mother could never have afforded the small mausoleum they had built just for him. Stacey was sure it had been paid for by Robert Golsch, the billionaire businessman. He came to the gravesite also, but he stood alone, far back from the others, across a vast carpet of quiet green studded with smaller gravestones. Stacey stood back also, but not half so far as Golsch, as if she felt one less degree of guilt and shame.

Roland's widow Frieda was at the graveside. Stacey had betrayed her former friend Frieda by starting an affair with her husband, then agreeing to become his second wife. Stacey wished she could explain to Frieda how Roland had forced her into that position. Roland had even required Frieda to participate in his wedding to Stacey. The ceremony had been almost as humiliating to Frieda as it had been to Stacey. Then, the ceremony had been disrupted, and Roland had been killed outside the church. Frieda was obviously grieving now. Her tall figure was stooped as she cried into her hands. This was no time to approach her with excuses.

But she had to approach Golsch. She was going to have to deal with him sooner or later. He was standing alone, squinting into the sun. He was tall and vaguely handsome, blonde hair going grey. He pressed his handkerchief under his gold, wire-rimmed glasses. As Stacey turned from the gravesite and slowly approached him, she thought she saw him wipe away tears.

She spoke very quietly. "Mr. Golsch, I'm Stacey Davenport. I'm really sorry for your loss." Even though he must have seen her slowly walking towards him over the long grassy expanse of the cemetery, Golsch looked startled. He jammed his hands into his coat pockets.

"My loss?" His stare at her was hard.

"I know," she spoke as softly as she could. "I know why you're here."

Golsch had never admitted that he was Roland's father. Stacey knew he had tried over the years to make up for it with money, and by supporting Roland's political career. Roland had been grateful for the political help, but their relationship had always been strained. Golsch had been worse than stand-offish, and he was paying the price now as he grieved totally alone.

"He told me," she met his stare. "He told me you're his father. He was your only child. I am so sorry for your loss."

Roland had confessed to her not only his father's identity, but also the full history of his father's twisted, secret love.

There were all kinds of love, but there seemed to be only one kind of grief. She could see the suffering in his eyes. She imagined how awful it must be to have to stand back and pretend you were a stranger at your own son's funeral.

"He could have been a great man," she offered.

She waited for a response, but Golsch just stared at her. Roland had been much better looking than his father, but Stacey could see the resemblance in the strong jaw and the penetrating blue eyes. "I really believe he could have been a great man, and ...."

He stopped her short. "If not for you, he'd be alive today."

Stacey took a breath. Was this what everybody thought about her? It was time to set the record straight. "That's not fair. I had nothing to do with his death."

"You agreed to marry him and be his second wife. Why?"

Stacey held his gaze. "I didn't have a choice. He said if I didn't become his second wife, he would sign off on that horrible law, MOMS, and my sister, and thousands of other women in Kansas, would be taken into captivity. You should know that. You were supporting that law."

"He didn't tell me that part, that part about you." Golsch's eyes were downcast now, the lines on his face more pronounced. "I offered him the governorship if he would support that bill. But he chose you over me. And that's why he's dead."

Stacey swallowed back her rising anger. But she wasn't going to take the blame for the tragedy that was Roland's death. She planted herself right in front of him and tried to stare him down. "No. He's dead because he lost his bearings. He's dead because he went into a jealous fit and needed to control everything that I did, everything I said, or thought. He's dead because you taught him people exist only to be controlled." Then she stormed away.

But he called after her. "Ms. Davenport. Ms. Davenport?" She didn't turn, but she could feel him coming after her. His looming figure appeared suddenly at her side, and she felt the sudden rush of his powerful presence. They were walking side by side, but his voice was now hushed. "He told me you were pregnant. I should have called you then." Intrigued by his apparent apology, she slowed to steal a sidewise glance.

"Roland would have been a great dad," she lied. She felt it was worth a lie to keep from hurting this man any more. She had lost any desire to hurt him.

"Do you know if it will be a boy or a girl?"

"A girl."

His frown disappeared. She thought she saw a trace of a smile.

"I wonder who she'll look like."

Stacey didn't get it at first. Then she did. He thought it was Roland's child. He was thinking he was going to be a grandfather.

She shrugged. "Well, you never know. I look exactly like

my mother, so maybe the baby'll look exactly like me. Too bad for her, I guess." She forced a laughed and turned away. She couldn't bear to tell him it wasn't Roland's child. Not here. Not at his only son's funeral.

She went back and took her place, alone, on the other side of the mourners from Golsch. It looked like his hands were shaking. She saw him frantically fumbling for something in his pocket. There was something both strange and familiar about his movements. She had a feeling she should know what they meant, but she couldn't put her finger on it. She kept watching him through the rest of the service.

Neither of them was invited to join the other mourners when the ceremony was over. After Roland's widow, and his mother, and the crowd of close friends and political allies gradually trickled away, the disgraced fiancée and the unacknowledged father stood facing each other across an empty stretch of sloping green grass with the gravesite in between them. Golsch had looked more and more disturbed as the ceremony dragged on. Now, without making eye contact with her, he put an obviously shaking hand to his face. Something fell to the ground. Stacey recognized it. She knew what was going on. It took one to know one.

He turned and began to walk away on another path, but she caught up with him. "You forgot this." She held up the torn slip of silver and purple foil.

"I don't know what that is." He tried to turn to walk away, but he suddenly stopped. He stood unmoving, an awful grimace on his face. As he pulled a shaky hand from his pocket, another silver and purple packet fell to the ground. Stacey reached down and snapped it up, looked at it closely.

"Naloxone and buprenorphine. You shouldn't need two of these packets." From long experience, Stacey knew all the drugs associated with addiction, and recovery, and maintenance.

"Give it to me!" Golsch grabbed her wrist, his hands weak but his voice still somehow commanding. She handed it over to him. He turned away and squeezed the contents into his mouth.

She waited and watched. Gradually, he seemed to relax, but he seemed too weak to walk.

"You shouldn't need two. You shouldn't be self-medicating so much," she practically shouted at him. He turned and tried to walk away, but his legs were wobbly. Soon he bent down toward the grass in obvious pain. She moved to stand in front of him. The cemetery was deserted now but for the two of them. It was a long walk across the grass to the nearest road. "I'm calling 911."

"No!"

"You need help."

"I can take care of myself."

"Said the addict. I have a lot of experience with this. I can get you help."

"I have the best doctors in the world, Ms. Davenport."

"I'm not leaving you alone." Besides the fact that he was a man in pain, she now recognized so many strange connections between them she couldn't just walk away.

A reflexive mask of cold calculation suddenly settled on his features as he stared at her from his crouched position like an angry gnome. "What do you want?"

"I want you to get medical help, now. That's all I want."

"Roland always said you helped him." He spoke behind clenched teeth.

"I'm calling 911."

"No!" He reached up and violently grabbed her hand, almost dragging her off her feet. He pulled her down so strongly she had to crouch down herself to keep from falling. Then he reached into his suit pocket with his other hand and pulled out his phone. "Dial the number for Doctor Gibbs! Only that number! It's my doctor. Nobody else."

She dialed as he told her to. "This is Robert Golsch," he demanded of whoever answered the phone. "I'm at Mount Hope Cemetery. Get Doctor Gibbs out here at once. This is an emergency. Dr. Gibbs. Nobody else. Right now."

After she hung up and he managed to put the phone away, Stacey stood and helped him stand. They shuffled off together to a large rectangular gravestone, where they sat on the cold granite, side by side.

"You can go now, Miss Davenport."

"I'm not going anywhere until the doctor arrives."

"I'm not an addict. It's just prescriptions. I took a couple extra this morning because I knew this day would be hard."

"Every day is hard, isn't it? I know that feeling well." His eyes met hers for a second with a flash of what she hoped was insight before he bent down again in pain. She stayed until the doctor arrived in a Golsch Industries limousine that ploughed right over the grass between the tombstones.

Chapter 7

Eleni's dark, serious eyes and resonant voice lent her opinions more weight than those of the typical first-year legal assistant. Grant found himself drawing out their conversations just to listen to her worldly-wise take on things. He noticed Eleni seemed to have the same effect on Jeanine, the office manager, and some of the other workers. Eleni didn't talk about her personal life, her goals, or her ambitions. And the company rules followed Massachusetts state regulations, under which it was forbidden for a supervisor to ask a personal question of an employee. Grant was relieved at first that he didn't have to engage in any idle chit-chat with her. He was swamped with work when she first came, and he just wanted somebody to take some of it off his desk.

When he came back from a two-week-long stint deposing witnesses in Chicago and Los Angeles, he had expected a backlog of legal problems to be piled up on his desk. One of the constantly recurring problems Liotech faced was litigation over patents. There were many companies that bought up reams of old patents, sight unseen, just so they could sue small companies with bogus claims to extort money. Liotech had two new internet security projects, and they were going so well they were being sued about once a month for patent or copyright infringement. He hadn't had time to keep up while he was out of town.

"New lawsuit," was the totality of Jeanine's greeting as he stepped into the office on his first day back from Los Angeles.

"It's nice to see you, too, Jeanine."

"Right. Amos didn't know what to do. He couldn't reach you, so he just gave it to Eleni and told her to do what she could with it."

"What! He gave it to a first-year legal assistant?"

He rushed into his office to see what the damage was. His desktop was clean and organized. He'd asked Eleni to try to keep up with his correspondence, so he wasn't too surprised at that.

What did surprise him were the documents that Eleni had left on the top of his desk. The legal complaint filed against Liotech was there, and Grant picked it up right away. Another patent infringement case. Underneath those papers was a cover memo Eleni had written analyzing the case. He sat reading it for half an hour. She had already done much of the hard work on the case. She had researched this area of the law, figured out the legal claim, consulted with Liotech's people about the technical merits of the case, and recommended a strategy as to how to proceed. She recommended they file a motion to dismiss in federal court. Grant smirked when he read this. He knew this was easier said than done.

Then he noticed she had already done it. A separate document, Eleni's proposed motion to dismiss, was right underneath the analysis. Eleni had not only set out the exact motion to be filed but also had attached affidavits, documents and scientific studies sufficient to convince almost any judge that conducting a trial on this issue would be a complete waste of the court's time.

"This is fantastic, awesome," he told her when she appeared at the door to his office. He motioned her in and asked her to sit down. "How much time did you spend on this?"

"A lot. There was nobody here to ask, except the IT people. They put me in the ball park, as far as the coding was concerned." Her eyes looked tired.

"I'll have to go over this with a fine-tooth comb, of course, but it looks very good."

"Thanks," she sighed. She seemed to be glad to be turning the case over to him.

"Honestly, I wish you were as excited about this case as

I am now. I think you really might have a future in this type of litigation."

"Oh." She seemed embarrassed. "They told me you lost a lot of time last summer helping out on that political campaign in Kansas. Fighting the good fight. Then you had to do those depositions in LA. I thought you needed my help on this." She paused, screwed up her mouth. "But, you know, this is not what I want to do with my life."

He knew he wasn't allowed to ask any personal questions, but he really wanted to know. "What is it that you do want to do with your life, Eleni?"

He couldn't figure out the look in her eyes. Startled? Defiant? "I don't want to say." She went on, her voice now low, calm. "I don't think it's something you would understand."

* * * * * *

Eleni had never continued the conversation about what she wanted in life, and he had no right to ask. So, he had to guess what powered her devotion to the law. He started to believe there was some mysterious passion lying dormant behind those intelligent eyes. But he was not allowed to ask. The whole thing bothered him more than it should have. He wanted to know more about her.

Grant was not the kind of person who would remain in an uncomfortable personal relationship for long. He sent a letter to Eleni's home address enclosing a blank PR-26 form. PR-26 was a form that the personnel department of every employer was required to keep on file. It was used to give notice to management that two employees had begun a personal relationship, so the employer could be on the lookout for favoritism or conflicts of interest. But Grant also enclosed a short letter. In that letter, he explained that he had signed the form simply because he wanted the chance to discuss her plans for her professional future. It was the only way he could legally do it, he explained. If she would also sign the form, they could have this conversation without violating Massachusetts law.

Eleni wrote a one-sentence reply to his home: *What? No CTS form?*

Grant had always carried one of these Consent To Sex forms in his wallet in college, and he had made good use of them. But what had he gotten himself into now? Was Eleni being sarcastic, or what? He agonized for hours over what he should write back, eventually deciding he'd just have to confront her in person. He decided he'd ask her to go to a coffee shop after work – not a date, and with each paying their own way.

Instead, they found themselves alone at the conference table in his office early the next day. Amos had called a meeting between the three of them but had been abruptly called away. Eleni stood up to go. He could see she was strictly adhering to the state's rules against personal interactions between supervisor and employee. She turned toward the door without a word about the letters they had sent to each other's homes. He decided her comment about the CTS form had probably been just sarcasm.

"Eleni, could you stay back for a minute? Maybe close the door."

She turned and met his eyes, her look questioning, skeptical. She deftly pushed the door behind her shut with the heel of her shoe. The echo of the tiny click of the latch in that silent room unnerved him. He stood up and retreated behind the conference table.

"I need to apologize for my letter," he began. "I think you might have gotten the wrong idea."

"Oh." She raised her eyebrows.

"I want to apologize," he offered now. "I don't even know now why I started our ... *correspondence*."

"You don't?" There was a smile in her voice.

"No. I mean yes, I did it because I was interested in you."

"That's what those forms are for." Was there a trace of sarcasm in her voice? Even mockery?

"No. I mean …."

She walked around the table and stood in front of him. Despite her bold move, the look in her eyes was tentative. She didn't seem to know what to do with her hands. She wasn't too close to him, but her body language was clear.

"I was so happy you sent me that form!" she said. "I had no idea you were interested in me." She met his eyes, tentatively, but with a trace of a smile on her lips. She seemed to be trying to catch a smile from him.

He kept a straight face and put his hands up to ward her off. He wanted to explain that he thought she was brilliant and that he was just interested in her career plans. Then a hint of a lilac scent drifted up from her hair. Her earrings sparkled. He dared to look into her eyes, study that earnest, upturned face. Her lips seemed to be inviting his. It had been a long time since he'd been that close to a woman. What was he saving himself for?

Eleni pulled back from his first chaste, tentative kiss. "I didn't dare dream you wanted me. But I think you sent me the wrong form. You will sign a Consent to Sex form, won't you? I have one with me."

His heart was racing. He thought he would drown in her scent. She had to be able to tell how much he wanted her. But he pushed her away. "Let's go outside. Not on the work premises."

"Please, sign the damn form!"

"Sure. Sure. Yes. Give it to me."

"The door has a lock."

✳✳✳ ✳✳✳

They registered with Liotech as "partners in a relationship." This put Human Relations on guard against any favoritism. The issue of favoritism was hardly a problem. There was no one else he could favor. But every action by Grant that had anything to do with Eleni had to be viewed with skepticism. Even so, it really wasn't much of a problem. The two of them were the entire legal department, they still worked well together, and they got their work done even more efficiently than before.

Eleni would sometimes touch him when they were alone at work, brushing her fingertips on his arm or across the back of his hand. She always gave him a quick, conspiratorial glance to see if he was aroused, or if he noticed at all. He sometimes was aroused, especially if she held eye contact for too long. He didn't think this behavior was appropriate or productive in the workplace, but he loved it. After that first day, the next place they made love was in her apartment. Her roommate was studying in the bedroom next door. He had hoped for a little more privacy, but it just worked out that way. He didn't mention his discomfort with the arrangement. He didn't want to seem like a stick in the mud. He had forgotten how young she was.

He had almost forgotten how young he was himself. He knew he would enjoy this woman. Romance was fun again, and free.

Chapter 8

Although she had no way to keep track of the days, Renee guessed she had been captive for about a month. While the Genesis Riders were first deciding what to do with her, she had succeeded for a while in making herself so obnoxious none of them came near her. But that didn't last. One night they forced drugs down her throat, and she lost all sense of time and place and even who she was. She remembered being on a bed in a room with guys. She hurt the next day. All she could do was hope nothing happened that would injure her child. Her expectation that her boyfriend would quickly find her faded as day after day went by and she was moved from place to place.

They sold her to a farmer in the western part of the state. He told her he was fifty-three, had been married once for about a year, thirty years ago, and had no children. He did most of his own work, but he hired field hands on a seasonal basis who lived in a long, low bunkhouse fifty yards behind his own house. He told her she didn't have to live in the bunkhouse; she would live in the "big house" with him. The big house was a one-story clapboard affair, originally a two-bedroom. Various owners had patched additional rooms onto the sides and the back over the years so haphazardly you could almost use any room for any function. The farmer had used most of the rooms as storage bins for his collection of machinery he was never going to fix. Although he owned her, and she knew what he wanted from her, she pretended she was just a servant and kept busy and moved around fast and made herself scarce for any other activities. But one day he made her go out to the chicken coop where she watched him wrench the head off a hen. Then he insisted she watch while he demonstrated what he could do with one of his machines.

"People have been cut up in these wood chippers. Pieces so small no one ever found a trace." He stared into her eyes then. He wasn't a talkative man. This was the only explanation she would ever get. She felt her insides go weak.

But it was only a few days later that a small horde of Genesis Riders approached the house, accompanied by the sheriff's car. The Riders revved their motors and raced around the house, tearing up the vegetable garden, while the sheriff knocked on the door.

"This auctioning off of these girls, it can't happen," Sheriff Weakins began. "Reverend Ezekial and I both agree – me because it's illegal, and Ezekial because he says that's not the way God wants it done. You got to give her back. She's got to be brought back to Neola City to be assigned by the clergy there."

"I paid these guys good money for her. Fifteen hundred dollars. Fair and square."

"Yeah, I know you made a deal. That's why I brought Hunter and the rest of these Riders with me, so they can see you're giving her back and so I can see that you get back your money."

"What kind of chickenshit Indian-giving deal is this?"

"Shut your mouth. Hand over the girl." Hunter's voice was deep, his scowl menacing as he stepped between the other two men. He was a huge, muscled, tattooed man, the tattoos fading and spreading but the muscles more exaggerated as middle age approached. His bald, bullet-shaped head was decorated with a tattoo of a snake about to strike.

The farmer put his hand on the back of Renee's neck and slowly pushed her toward the two men. She didn't ask to go back and get her things. She didn't really own anything anyway. She walked toward the sheriff's car, but he pointed her toward Hunter. He told her to get on his bike. There was no point in resisting. She climbed on behind him. He didn't handcuff or zip tie her to the machine. She'd have to hang on to him somehow, though her arms couldn't reach far around him.

Hunter waved an open envelope stuffed with cash at the sheriff. The sheriff nodded, started his car, forced his way through the crowd of cyclists, made a U-turn, forced his way through the crowd again and powered his way down the dusty road back to Neola City. The farmer walked up to Hunter's cycle and asked for his money. Hunter handed him the envelope full of bills.

"Wait! This is only seven-fifty. You owe me fifteen hundred."

"Yeah. Well, there's a restocking fee." Hunter laughed, revved his engine, and sped off, followed by the rest of the gang.

* * * * * *

Even if her voice could be heard over the roar of the engine, there was no point in asking where they were going. She knew she wasn't free. She heard the sheriff say she would be assigned to someone by the clergy. She hoped, if a church were involved, her boyfriend Jeff would at least be told where she was taken. But she really had no idea. Renee was twenty-three and had never paid any attention to what was going on in the world other than in her father's home and among their neighbors and church friends. She got most of her information from her church and from her father's incessant preaching. Her father was a devotee of Reverend Ezekial. His radio sermons and political podcasts echoed through the house day and night. Ezekial's voice was a kind of background theme to her life, but she never really listened to what he was saying because she figured her father would tell her any part of it she needed to know.

Her father controlled every detail of her life. He treated

her little sister Ruth the same way. He was so infuriated when Renee took a job outside the house that he refused to drive her there. She was not allowed to have a license, so she rode the family's aging mare to the job the first day. It was three miles away. Her father beat her for that when she returned. After that, she walked every day – at least as far as around the first bend, where Jeff picked her up. Her father refused to talk to her, except for preaching.

His self-righteous anger burned white hot six months later when he found out Jeff had gotten her pregnant. Jeff had befouled her in the eyes of God, he said. But she could tell he was looking forward to Jeff taking the responsibility for her off his shoulders. Jeff was her first boyfriend, and he got her pregnant on their first date. She was eager to marry him and get out of that house. She had always supposed she had to hitch herself to some man, and Jeff was a lot nicer than her father.

When the Genesis Riders first came for her, her father told her only that she would be hitched to a better, more God-fearing man. Already zip tied before they even got her off the front porch, she begged to be allowed to go back inside and say goodbye to Ruth. Her father said he hadn't realized Ruth was eligible, too. So they took Ruth, too. It had never been any secret that Ruth was her father's favorite. Renee thought she saw a flicker of remorse in her father's eyes when they dragged Ruth out. None for her, though.

They blindfolded both sisters. When she arrived at the clubhouse and they took off her blindfold, Ruth wasn't there. She hadn't seen her since. After the night she was drugged, two other women came, and they shared a mattress on the floor of one of the upstairs bedrooms. They were tied up only at night. One morning, she tried to convince one of the Riders that God would prefer that she marry the man who was the father of her child, but he just told her to shut up.

"Don't you understand?" one of the other women, Moira, said to her that night. "They don't give a shit about God, or the Bible. They're thugs. They're auctioning us off on the internet to the highest bidder."

"You're kidding."

"No, I'm serious. I heard them arguing. About you, actually. They said you're worth a lot less pregnant."

Moira told her there was some new law that said unmarried women who were not chaste could be taken from their homes. "It's some kind of religious shit."

"Don't say 'shit.' Religion is not shit."

"Well, this is shit. We're slaves now. Bought and sold."

Renee came to understand that the Genesis Riders were just outlaws who were using the religious laws for their own benefit. But now that the clergy would be deciding where she went, she hoped she would be reassigned to a better man. She now knew that these men had to be already married. At least that meant she'd have some other woman to talk to. And maybe that woman wouldn't think being pregnant was such a freakish sin.

She was taken to an interview with Ezekial himself. She was amazed that the Rider who took her to his office barged right in, showing the holy man little respect. She stood straight, feeling guilty for the shabby and filthy clothes she was wearing. But Ezekial didn't even look up. He abruptly asked her how many children she had.

"None." She tried to keep the tremor out of her voice. "But I am three months pregnant."

He smiled. She knew he had a lot of children because he mentioned it often in his sermons. Ezekial slowly tapped a pencil on his desk. He wasn't really looking at her. "Do you have any skills? I mean office skills, accounting, correspondence, computer software?"

"My job was keeping track of the billing."

Ezekial continued to search for answers from above. Then he made his decision. "Give her to Prescott. His wife is barren."

She was ushered out and immediately deposited in Prescott's home. His wife answered the door. She seemed to be in her mid to late thirties, dark haired, well dressed. She looked shocked by Renee's shabby appearance, and she sniffed at the air as if her smell was just as bad.

"Here she is," is all the Rider had to say.

"I'm Renee," Renee said, hoping against hope to start things off on the right foot.

"I understand you've already been screwing around and got yourself pregnant."

"I am pregnant."

"I am pregnant, *Ma'am*!"

"I am pregnant, Ma'am."

"Don't ever forget who is the first wife. You, Rider, can't you get her cleaned up before you leave her here?"

"No." He turned and walked away.

Mr. Prescott was more welcoming. He took away her ragged clothes while she was in the shower and left some of his wife's old clothes for her to wear. She didn't know if she should thank him, but decided she should. He seemed kind, and he showed her to her own bedroom. But Mrs. Prescott slapped her the instant she saw the clothes.

"What? Mr. Prescott gave them to me. Should I take them off? I don't know where my old ones are."

"I guess if he said to wear them, wear them."

She spent the night in fear of how her child would be treated by Mrs. Prescott. Mr. Prescott didn't come to her room that night, and she wondered if he wanted a child more than a concubine. Or maybe he was too afraid of Mrs. Prescott to start right in on the new wife. It didn't seem like it was going to be a happy household.

But that was her last night with the Prescotts. The next day, a different Genesis Rider appeared at the door and said he was taking her back to Reverend Ezekial. "He says you'll get a new one," he told Mrs. Prescott.

Mr. Prescott wasn't home. His wife did the talking. "What is this? A fucking revolving door?"

"Ha! Guess it is. Hand her over. Ezekial's orders."

She pushed Renee out the door. He zip tied her wrists.

"Give me my clothes back," Mrs. Prescott demanded. "She's wearing my clothes."

He stopped, looked at Renee's clothes, looked at Renee's tied wrists, then led her away. "Take it up with your husband," he called back over his shoulder.

Chapter 9

During her campaign, Stacey had been called a drug addict, an adulteress, a voluntary concubine, and worse. There was a kernel of truth to all of these allegations. But her story was more complex. The final humiliation forced on her by Roland was her agreement to marry him as his second wife. This had actually been an act of self-sacrifice on her part on behalf of all the other women in Kansas. Most of the women in Kansas recognized that. But many others put the blame on her. Reverend Ezekial preached on almost a daily basis that she was a fiendish succubus who had left Roland with no choice but to try to put her into servitude. Roland's death at the end of the truncated wedding ceremony was still being investigated. Nobody knew exactly what to think of Stacey now.

Her plan was to use the political skills she had learned from Roland to unite the Independents once again and hold out against any further attempts by the Certainty Party to drag women back into bondage. Stacey started with Martha Smarks, her suitemate in the legislature in Topeka. In their very first conversation, however, Martha had gone into a such an intense reverie about Roland that Stacey couldn't snap her out of it. But Stacey knew no one else. She had to try again.

"Martha, can we talk about just politics, just for now? How things stand? I mean, what's next, now that MOMS has been defeated?" Martha didn't have much choice but to listen. Stacey was in Martha's office, sitting on the chair right beside Martha's desk. "We need to repeal some of these other brutal laws that the Certainty Party has passed. Did you know my sister was branded?"

"Oh, I heard. I'm sorry. Really, I am so sorry. She is just a teenager, I know. But do you really think we can get the votes to repeal the Branding of Felons and Addicts Act?"

The branding law applied to all convicted recidivist felons and habitual addicts. The language was a little vague. So far, the government hadn't seemed to notice people like Stacey, whose fight with addiction seemed to be over years ago and who were successfully pursuing careers. In any case, no one had dared propose branding her, or any of the other law students. So, some addicts were branded and some were not. But the law was sloppy in the other direction, too. Stacey's sister Amy was neither a felon nor an addict, but she had been branded by the Genesis Riders anyway, just for fun.

The Certainty Party supported the branding law because of their belief that there were two distinct kinds of people – good, God-fearing people, and bad people – and that the state should help the good people by clearly marking the bad. The bill had passed the legislature by a slim majority, receiving only a few votes from anybody outside the CP. Most people had assumed that their mild-mannered governor, "Sweet Fanny" Adams, would veto it. But Governor Adams had been running scared of the CP at the time and, to the surprise of all, she signed the bill.

But the whole dynamic of the legislature had changed since Stacey's election. Stacey and her allies could muster a little more than one-third of the legislature against any CP bill, thus assuring the good governor that her vetoes would stick. Governor Adams was beginning to show a backbone. But Stacey now hoped to get a majority of the legislature to vote to repeal the branding law. She had no doubt that if a majority of the legislature voted to repeal the law now, Governor Adams would sign the repeal bill. And if this happened, she could stop worrying about getting branded herself.

"But how are you going to get the bill through the legislature? The CP still has a majority," Martha persisted.

"I don't know." Stacey was frank. "Hope for a miracle?"

Martha smirked. "I've never found hoping for a miracle to be a strong legislative plan."

Their conversation was interrupted by Angela, who served as legislative aide to both Stacey and Martha. Angela was normally a meek, quiet soul, but she barged right into the room after knocking. "Martha, I hate to interrupt, but Bill Biftek said he wants to meet with you outside the governor's office. He says it's urgent."

"Biftek?" Martha repeated the name of Golsch's main lobbyist in Topeka. "What in the world would he want with me?"

William "Bud" Biftek was the primary lobbyist for Robert Golsch's business interests. Everybody in Topeka knew him. He was a large, affable, friendly man, a hard man to dislike. He had such a comprehensive knowledge of what was going on that legislators often came to him for advice about what a bill might mean, or who it might affect. But he rarely had any need of the Independents, and they rarely talked to him. But if Biftek wanted to talk, only a fool would refuse to listen.

"I guess I'd better go," Martha apologized, and Stacey nodded in agreement.

Two minutes after Martha was out of the suite, Stacey heard a soft knock on her door. She jumped to see Robert Golsch standing in the doorway, looking awkward and out of place.

"Oh! Mr. Golsch! Are you looking for Bill Biftek? He called for Martha a few minutes ago. I think they went to the governor's office."

"No. I'm here to see you, Stacey."

* * * * * *

Stacey understood why Martha had to go when Biftek called. Stacey had learned already that there were almost no "real people" at the capital in Topeka. People who worked hard all day at their jobs almost never had the time or the knowledge to approach their delegates and ask for relief from their real problems. Most legislative issues were perceived by the delegates as disputes between lobbyists. Lobbyists were the people that really had to be listened to.

"What did Biftek want?" she asked Martha when she returned twenty minutes later.

"I don't get it," Martha shook her head. "There's going to be some rinky-dink little ceremony that Biftek is setting up to honor Governor Adams on her birthday. He wanted my advice on the speakers' list. I have no idea why he needed me for that."

Stacey figured it out right away, but she would never tell Martha. Biftek's only purpose had been to get Martha out of the suite long enough for Golsch to make his request of Stacey in secret. Stacey was now emboldened to push Martha harder on the issue.

"Martha, can't we make it an Independent priority to repeal the Branding of Felons and Addicts Act?"

"Stacey, that has to be a frightening thing for you." By starting off with a personal comment about Stacey's feelings, Martha demonstrated she had the skills of a true politician. "I know you haven't taken any drugs for years, but they could still brand you now, because you're still technically an addict. And they probably would have, if you hadn't won the election."

"I'll always be an addict. And there's no exceptions in the law for recovering addicts. Or for legislators."

"I know. It's awful. It's so awful. But Stacey, all the Independents, even together with all the sensible Republicans and Democrats, make up just a little over a third of the legislature. Thanks to you, we can uphold Governor Adams' veto of any new, crazy CP legislation, but we still can't get a majority for any bills of our own."

"I know. I know. But what if I could get Golsch to support us?"

Martha shook her head slowly. "I know you're new to the legislature. But I thought you understood. Golsch hates us. We helped kill his bill abolishing the minimum wage." She peered at Stacey as if she were dismayed that Stacey couldn't understand these simple concepts. "To tell the truth, he has reason to hate you more than anybody. You're the one who administered the *coup de grace* to his legislative plan."

Stacey flinched. There was so much that Martha didn't know, and she hated not being able to tell her. But the bottom line was, neither of the two women really trusted each other fully yet. Stacey understood now that, deep down, Martha still resented her affair with Roland. Roland might have ultimately been a failure as a man, but he had come close enough to political greatness to have left his mark on a lot of souls, including Martha's.

"What if I told you that Golsch does not hate me, and he told me he has an open mind about repealing the Branding of Felons and Addicts Act?"

"That can't be true." Martha stared at her intently, a suspicious look showing in her otherwise innocent blue eyes.

"What if I'm absolutely sure he will support repeal? That doesn't guarantee it will pass, but it might give us a chance. What do I have to do to get the Independent Party to put this at the top of their agenda?"

Martha glared at her. "What did you have to *do* to get that kind of commitment out of Golsch." She emphasized each word separately, like a scolding teacher.

"It's complicated, Martha. And it's a secret. I think I can guarantee his support. If you don't want to carry this message to the Independent Party, Martha, I'll do it myself. But it would be so much better if we went together."

Martha finally agreed. Stacey was still greeted with enough

suspicion at the Independent Party caucus that she decided to let Martha do all the talking. They were in a currently unused hearing room in the House. The microphones weren't working, and Martha had to shout to be heard by the fifty or so delegates who were present.

"What does Golsch want in return?"

"Nothing. He's giving up totally on repealing the minimum wage. He saw that study. Most businesses his size pay more than the minimum wage anyway. His bill would have only have helped the tiny businesses, and Golsch doesn't give a shit about them."

"He had to know that all along," someone shouted.

"Of course, he knew. It was just symbolic for him. I think he was dreaming of becoming president. Repealing the minimum wage would have been his Far Right catchphrase that would have gotten him the support of every rich Neanderthal in the country."

"But what are our assurances Golsch will support repeal of the branding law? He supported branding just a year ago when that law passed."

"Here's your assurance." Martha spoke calmly, so everybody had to listen. "Your assurance is me. I give you my absolute assurance that Golsch will support repeal."

It worked. No one had ever before seen Martha so confident of anything. The few delegates who grumbled that someone must be sleeping with Golsch were stared down by other delegates who had worked with Martha in the past. In the end, the caucus voted to put in a bill to repeal the Branding of Felons and Addicts Act. The caucus chose Martha to sponsor the repeal bill even though she didn't have the experience that some other Independents had. This also put the whole responsibility on her shoulders if the whole effort collapsed.

Stacey followed her all the way back to her office. "Thank you."

"I didn't want to put any of the responsibility on you," Martha explained. "You're an unknown quantity. They might not have trusted you."

"But you trusted me. You took my word. That means a lot to me."

Chapter 10

New Height with Friends *vinyl available Thursday 8:30 p.m.*

It was only two days after their first meeting with Damien at the record store that Amy received the text, sent to her brother Kendrick's phone. A text from male to male was less likely to be tapped by Conception Control. And the code, sent to Kendrick, a budding rapper, sounded innocuous. But Amy was peeved that the code was incomplete.

Should I bring cash?

Cash preferred.

They hadn't been tracked the last time they drove to the record store, and there were no repercussions from that trip. The coded message from Damien meant to come at 8:30 that evening. *Cash preferred* meant to bring Ruth.

They drove to the record store building, passed it by slowly, made a U-turn, came back, then drove around behind it, each time craning their necks to make sure there was no customer in there with Damien. They parked in the back and walked around to the front of the store. Not a single vehicle had passed since they first came within sight of the building. Damien let them in quickly, keeping one eye on the road. "I've got a surprise for you, Amy," he crowed.

Her father appeared in the hallway from the restroom with a huge smile on his face. Amy ran toward him and practically jumped into his arms.

"Oh, little girl, I missed you."

She held his hug for a while before saying anything. "Dad, I'm so glad you're okay." She stood back, still touching his arm with her hand, and studied his face. Suddenly, she put her other hand up and traced the mark on his forehead with her thumb. Then he did the same to her. "Losers together forever, huh, Dad."

"We're going to be okay, honey."

She leaned in and put both palms against his chest, demanding the attention of the man who had neglected her all of her life. "Dad, Stacey says you should come out in the open. It makes you look guilty that you disappeared right after Roland was killed."

"If the police find me and ask me for a statement, I'll tell them the truth."

"But where are you living? Not here. Not in that apartment upstairs."

"No. I'm not coming back here, not after those two addicts were killed out back. You all can stop paying the rent."

"You should come home," Amy pleaded.

"They burned that down."

"I mean, Mom's going to rent a more permanent house next month. You should come home then."

He just nodded. Amy could see he didn't agree. The room suddenly went silent. He seemed to notice Ruth for the first time.

"Hi, Ruth. I see you're packing heat."

"Always."

"Amy, I'm not coming home. At least not right now. Please give my love to Stacey and Kendrick ... and your Mom. I think I can serve the resistance best if I stay in hiding in Neola County."

"Dad, Ruth wanted to ask you something, too."

Ruth's eyes opened wide like she hadn't expected to be asked to speak. "You rescued me. I'll never forget that." That was the easy part of her speech. But she was not used to asking for help, especially from men. She bowed her head slightly with the effort. "My sister was taken on the same day as me, and she's captured still. We need to rescue her."

"Where are they holding her?"

"That's the problem." Amy took over the conversation from Ruth. "We don't know. We thought you could help, Dad."

"Oh." Don seemed suddenly deflated. "I don't know if I can, honey. The word is, the women who were taken are now scattered all over the county."

Amy sighed. "So, you have no idea?"

"Um." Damien had been standing a little toward the side, keeping one eye out the window. "I might have some dope for you guys."

"What?" Both girls turned to him and spoke at once. Don also took a sudden interest in this skinny teenager.

"There's a couple Riders who come in here all the time. I hear them talking. Um, do you want me to say?"

"Of course, tell us. Please." All their eyes were on him. Ruth's eyes were sharp, Don's were skeptical. But Amy's eyes were pleading. Damien turned to her.

"Okay. They came in here about a week ago all mad. They said they were selling the girls like crazy on the internet, but then Ezekial and the sheriff made them take them all back. Made them pay back the money, too. Riders say they're poor now. That's their excuse now for making the record store owner pay protection money."

"So, the women are free now?" Ruth spoke directly to Damien for the first time since they arrived.

"No, no, that's not what I meant." Damien clapped his hands on either side of his head like he was desperately trying to keep the logic inside. "No. I mean, they had to take all the women back to Ezekial, over in Bible Land, and I guess he doles them out from there."

Don jumped in. "Okay. My guess is he'll keep a few for himself and hand out the rest to the married men in his congregation."

"Let's get there before he can give Renee away." Ruth

started pacing. "Stacey told us nobody's keeping records of where they're going. Once she's assigned, we'll never find her."

"Most of them are already assigned," Damien interjected.

"How do you know that?" Ruth gave him a suspicious glare. Was Damien trying to complicate things, discourage them from acting, like any coward would do?

"My father manages a slaughterhouse, United Processing. They use contract laborers sometimes, mostly for the dirty work. He's telling me all the time lately that these strange women are being bused in to work there. It's a contract labor service. They have these weird religious names. There's a church van that picks them up and brings them to the plant every day. They won't tell the managers their real names or addresses. They gotta be captives or concubines – whatever you call them."

Chapter 11

"How did you do that? How did you get these legislative magic powers?" Martha acted amazed, but still a little suspicious.

"My anti-branding bill only got assigned to committee. That's just the first step."

"Most Independent bills don't even get that far. Most of them die right at the Speaker's desk." Martha was impressed, even taken aback. She had come into Stacey's office once again and was sitting at the chair beside her desk. She liked Stacey and had told her so. She could tell that Stacey liked her. But Stacey's connection with Golsch was worrisome, and Stacey's secrecy about that was grating on Martha.

"I didn't do anything special. It just somehow got off the Speaker's desk and assigned to the Law Enforcement Committee." That wasn't the whole truth, of course, and Martha knew it – and Stacey knew that Martha knew it. Stacey believed that transparency was not always in her best interest. And, more importantly, revealing the secret she kept might blow up the whole plan.

"It's the personal connection, isn't it? I don't mean that disrespectfully. I know your sister was branded, and your family has suffered so much under the current law. Did you really get to the Speaker's heart? Does he have a heart?"

"I didn't even speak to the Speaker." Stacey immediately realized she shouldn't have said that. Martha had come up with a plausible reason for her success. She should have let Martha keep that idea in her head.

"Then Golsch obviously had something to do with this," Martha persisted. Then she took a deep breath. "Some of the men here are saying you sold yourself to him."

Stacey face suddenly turned red with rage. "Why would

you repeat that crap? You of all people should know better!"

Martha shrunk back in her little chair. "I'd appreciate it if you wouldn't yell at me."

"Sorry." Stacey put her head down on her desk until her breathing slowed down. Martha waited. "I'm sorry I yelled at you." Her voice was tiny now. "Sometimes it seems like nobody's on my side."

*** ***

When Bill Biftek showed up before the Law Enforcement Committee to speak about the repeal of the branding law, every delegate on the committee listened. Biftek rarely lied outright to the legislators, though he often shaded the truth. No legislator from any party ever pressed him on these shaded truths. They understood that an unfavorable word from him could result in a cut in Golsch's funding for their next campaign. Even the Independents were more than respectful to the man.

"My clients, Golsch Industries, the Golsch Broadcasting Network, the Kansas Chamber of Commerce, the United States Chamber of Commerce, Verizon, AT&T, and the Associated Meatpackers all support this bill, which would repeal the requirement that all convicted felons and those addicted to alcohol or controlled dangerous substances be branded on the forehead. We know the current branding law stemmed from good intentions, but that law has had grievous consequences for business. It has resulted in an unwillingness on the part of executives nationwide to relocate to Kansas. The unfair news coverage of the "barbaric branding frenzy," as it was called in the *New York Times*, might have been greatly exaggerated, but it has stymied the development of business in this state. My clients would like to compete on an equal footing with states that do not brand their citizens."

Translation: *Golsch wants this*. The Republicans and the

Democrats and the Independents now seemed to be leaning favorably toward the bill. A few Independents asked that their names be added as sponsors. But the Certainty Party, which held the majority of votes in the House and Senate, was not immediately on board. The chair of the committee, a Certainty Party leader, declined to bring the bill to a committee vote. The bill wasn't dead, but nothing was going to happen until the Certainty Party decided what to do.

"We have no leverage over the CP," Martha explained when the bill appeared to be stalled in committee. "They hate us Independents."

"But Golsch obviously wants this," Stacey replied. "He must think he has some way of making this happen."

"Maybe. I guess. Maybe he plans to do some deal with CP. But I bet we'll never find out what the deal is until it's too late."

"You're such an optimist," Stacey teased. In reality, she was starting to admire Martha's cold-eyed view of politics. For years, Stacey had watched her own mother whine and moan in despair over the state of politics in Kansas. She had seen that this whining and crying accomplished nothing. In contrast, Martha was on the front lines, looking the enemy straight in the eye, losing 90 percent of her battles but never giving up, always looking for ways to leverage her tiny bit of power to do a tiny bit of good. Martha was married with two children. She had a master's degree in public policy. Her husband was an accountant. She told Stacey she had run a shelter for battered women in Kansas City, but her experiences there led her to believe that the laws themselves were part of the problem. Stacey had never met a woman like her before.

"I really am an optimist," Martha smiled. "Look what's already happened. Golsch is supporting you, trying to repeal that barbaric branding law. Do you have any idea why?"

"No," Stacey lied.

*** ***

When Stacey went to the doctor's office for her next prenatal checkup, her insurance claim was rejected.

She sought out the administrator of the legislative health plan and found her staring at a computer screen in a tiny office in the basement of the building.

"I'm sorry, honey. There's an exclusion of prenatal care benefits for fornicators and adulterers."

The woman didn't look sorry.

Stacey tromped down the long underground corridors to her own suite. "I need a job with health insurance, what with the baby coming," she complained to Martha.

"Most legislators have regular jobs as well. But ...."

"But what?"

"I guess you haven't heard. The Certainty Party is now pushing a bill that will forbid any health plan from providing maternity health benefits for unmarried women. They say insurance companies are violating the religious rights of policyholders by paying benefits that reward sin."

Martha eased her way into Stacey's office and sat down on the chair beside her desk. She held Stacey's gaze. The afternoon sunlight barely edged its way through the small rectangular windows near the ceiling.

Martha hesitated. "Maybe I can get my doctor to see you for free. He's really nice. He's not an OB-GYN, but it would be better than nothing."

"Oh, that's really nice of you, but I don't think I'm there yet."

Martha sat straighter, sat closer, rested her arm on the edge of Stacey's desk. "Where exactly are you, Stacey?"

"What do you mean?"

Martha drummed her fingers on the desk right next to Stacey's hand. "I mean, you're carrying Roland's baby. Didn't he leave any money for you, or for the child?"

Stacey controlled her urge to push herself back in her chair and away from Martha. Did everybody think Roland was the baby's father? She was angry with herself. Why hadn't she told everybody the truth yet?

Martha took her silence as a no. "No money. Of course. You hadn't officially even become his second wife yet. So, yeah, there's absolutely no chance you'd be covered on his insurance policy."

Chapter 12

Grant asked Eleni not to do that any more, not to touch him at work even on the arm, even when they were totally alone. When he asked, she caught him with those quick brown eyes and nodded, almost humbly. And when she nodded, her hair slid forward, and she flipped it back, and Grant's heart skipped a beat. Although she had signed the CTS form and they were registered at Liotech as Partners in a Relationship, it was unclear whether such furtive touching on work time was a violation. Grant wanted their relationship to be completely above board and by the book, but they both had to fight for self-control.

Keeping from touching her all day just stoked his desire for her at night. She was only three years younger than Stacey, but sometimes she seemed like a kid to him. She gave herself eagerly to him in bed but looked away and gasped quietly at the end. She was never somber, even about love. She was too young for that.

"Sometimes I wish …." he said to her one night after sex, after they were both drained and satisfied and on the verge of sleep. "Wouldn't it be nice if you came to work at Liotech, too, after you graduate. It's technical, but also nice and down to earth. And we can talk to the actual owner whenever we want. And he's a great guy."

"I don't think so, Grant."

"But Liotech is exciting. We may all become millionaires – or have it all go down the tubes tomorrow. And I like working for real people who are my friends."

She just stared dreamily into his eyes until her lashes fluttered closed.

Eleni maintained her high level of efficiency at work, and she got along with everybody – even Jeanine, who had tried to get her kicked out with the ancestry thing. Grant was so enthralled by this unexpected affair that it took him a couple of weeks to get around to his original question to her: what did she want to do with her life? In bed one night he finally insisted on an answer.

"My mother was a refugee. From Cyprus. I know, you've probably never even heard of it. It's an island in the Mediterranean."

He was insulted. "I know about Cyprus."

"There was a war, or an almost-war, between Turkey and Greece over it. My mother got out, but her sister died in Hungary on the journey through Europe. My mother would have died except for the international relief agencies. I want to help them."

"So, you're not interested in the type of thing that Liotech does?"

"Oh, it's interesting ... but not really. I'm not criticizing what you do for a living. I'm sure it's got to be done. But my heart wouldn't be in it if I worked there full time."

"What would you actually do for a relief agency?"

"The United Nations does a lot of this work. And there are hundreds of smaller groups that are independent. They need to get in and out of countries. They need visas, cooperation agreements, organizational help, supply contracts. Long term, they need to negotiate international agreements. Maybe once in a while I could actually get on site and hand one meal to one hungry person."

Grant tried to hide his disappointment – in himself. He had had two serious girlfriends in his life. One hundred percent, two out of two, thought what he did for a living was not worth spending their own lives on. But he reminded himself that he really liked his job. And at least both of these women thought he was worthy of being a friend.

Friends with benefits, at times. The owner, Amos, had an

electronic lock installed on the door to the conference room. He handed Grant a narrow slip of paper.

"What's this?"

"It's the key code to the conference room door. I want to keep my two legal beagles as happy as possible. I know you two don't have much free time away from work." Amos walked away.

Grant brought her into the conference room when most of the employees were out eating lunch.

"What's this about? Where's everybody else?" She was always on top of things, always worried she might be missing something.

"Nobody else is coming. And Amos gave me the key code to lock the door."

Her eyes lit up. "You mean …? Right here?"

"Yup. If it's okay with you."

She looked around. There was no furniture in the room but the long table and a few awkward plastic chairs.

"I'm not an acrobat."

But he smiled to see the mischievous look in her eyes.

Chapter 13

The Rider transporting Renee stopped in front of Bible Land's high iron gate a few miles outside the town limits of Neola. The fence itself was made of black iron bars seven or eight feet high, with barbed wire loosely strung among the decorative *fleurs-de-lis* at the top. The fence stretched fifty yards on either side of the gate. After the Rider identified himself, the gate swung open to a wide green common with a row of large, identical, brick Georgian mansions on each side. The fence completely surrounded the houses and commons. Most of the houses were under construction; only the first two on the right were completely finished. The Rider took her to the first of these two.

"Delivery!" he yelled at the top of his voice. Renee had figured out by now that the Genesis Riders were not happy that the stolen women had to be retrieved and given to Ezekial to distribute. In her case, they were probably even more unhappy that they had to remove her twice, first from the farmer and then from the Prescotts. She had guessed that Mrs. Prescott ruled that roost back there.

"Get off," the Rider scowled, then took off without even cutting loose the zip ties.

Renee stepped carefully up the two steps to the portico and crossed it. She had to ring the doorbell with her nose. The door opened almost immediately. A young woman dressed in what looked like a Puritan costume, but with softer brown colors and a wide white lace collar, stared down at her with an almost pitying expression.

"Um, Ma'am, I think I'm supposed to be here. The Genesis Riders brought me."

"Oh. You'll have to be washed and dressed and oriented." The calmness with which this young girl uttered these bizarre things threw Renee off balance even more.

"Is this Reverend Ezekial's house? I think I'm just coming here so he can reassign me. My last, um … placement. I guess it didn't work out. My name's Renee, by the way. What's yours?"

"Dina." The girl opened the door wider and pointed inside. "Follow me. You must be washed and dressed."

The house was huge. Renee followed Dina down the long entrance hall, past what looked like a family room on the right. Two women dressed exactly like Dina were watching a baby and chasing after a couple of toddlers. Dina took her past the kitchen on the left. There was a long hall with doors on each side, each opening onto a small room with a single bed. At the end of the hall was a large bathroom with several sinks and two separate showers.

"Take your clothes off. Get in the shower. I'll bring you decent clothes. You have to be ready in ten minutes."

The clothes Renee had gotten from the Prescott's house didn't even fit, and she didn't mind getting rid of them. She supposed she'd have to wear the Puritan costume. She wondered how the assignment process worked. She wished she had some skill so she would not be stuck watching other women's kids all day and night. But she hoped she'd get to raise her own child when it was born. She was grateful for the chance to take a shower. She wished Dina were more talkative.

She dried her long red hair as best she could with a towel and combed it straight back. The clothes Dina brought her fit a little better, but she was taller than most women and everything was still a little short. She racked her brain to think of what she should do to get the best placement. She didn't want to be placed out on a farm again, alone with a nasty, uncommunicative farmer. She really didn't know what kind of servitude was best. The only thing she was sure of was she wanted to be somewhere where she would be able to raise her child, or at least watch it grow. But there wasn't any way to tell how she should act to make that happen.

Dina came and led her back down the corridor, through the kitchen and to a large room on the right set up like an office. "Sit here," she directed, pointing to a straight-backed wooden chair facing a large, cluttered desk. Dina said one more word, "Wait," then left.

Renee sat straight in the chair for fifteen minutes, but then she started to squirm. She stood up and walked around. A window on the wall to her right showed the outside brick walls of the corridor of bedrooms she had just walked through. A window behind the big desk looked out across a narrow green strip to the identical house next door. She leaned over the desk to see what she could see. Files, mostly closed files. She looked at the titles: "Sewerage" and "Zoning" were near the top. She couldn't read the rest without disturbing them, and she didn't dare do that. There was a flat desktop date calendar with scribbled notations all over it. There was a standing, nine-inch wooden cross glowing in the light from the window behind. But there was also a small, red, leather-bound book. It looked like a diary.

* * * * * *

"What are you doing?" She jumped at the sound of the Ezekial's voice, spoken low and practically in her ear. She didn't know what to say. She'd been caught red handed, snooping. She wanted to throw herself on his mercy, but she didn't know how. She dropped the book she had been looking at, stood up straight and backed away.

Even wearing flats, she was a little taller than the reverend. She slouched down a little to make herself seem shorter. She recognized him from seeing him preach on television and online: the round face, the thick, horn-rimmed glasses, the dyed brown comb over. He wasn't wearing his signature dark blue suit, and he looked a little heavier with his plain plaid shirt tucked under his tightly cinched belt. But none of that mattered. She knew he had complete power over her, body and soul. He continued to stare at her. She could feel beads of sweat rolling down her back. "Uh, I'm sorry, Reverend. I just got so bored waiting …." She backed away and sat down again in the wooden chair. Her situation hardly seemed real.

"Stand up again." She jumped to obey so fast she knocked down the chair behind her. Ezekial sat down behind the desk. "Turn around, slowly." She obeyed. He muttered something she couldn't understand, then suddenly jumped up. He came out from behind his desk and approached her, pushing her back a step with the palms of his hands.

"Take your clothes off."

She obeyed. Her body was covered with goosebumps, but she could feel her face was hot.

"Kneel."

She obeyed. She felt herself freezing up inside. This was how she was adjusting to being no longer being treated as a human. She was holding her breath, convincing herself it was somebody else, it wasn't really her who was kneeling on the floor being appraised like an animal. She didn't cry out for help, or even cry at all.

He walked slowly in a circle around her, kicking the chair out of the way. She felt his hand playing with her hair, pulling through it, letting it run through his fingers as he circled her again and again. It wasn't her hair, she told herself, it was someone else's hair. He could fondle it all her wanted. It had nothing to do with her.

Finally, Ezekial let go of her hair, stopped in front of her, squatted down and stared at her face. She met his eyes, as she had to, but she closed her mind so she could almost believe she wasn't seeing anything. He pushed his glasses up on his nose to study her better. A broad smile came over his face. "You look a lot like another woman who was taken and brought to me."

"My little sister. She looks just like me, but her hair's shorter. She was taken the same time as me. She wasn't even pregnant."

Ezekial's face molded itself into a smile of recognition. "Oh yes. I know. I know all about her."

"Do you know where she is? Do you think it's possible I could see her some time?"

"Tamar." Ezekial smiled at her benevolently. "That's your name now, Tamar. You can get up. Put your clothes on. You are lucky you were not entirely disobedient. Tamar, I'm assigning you to myself, as my sixth wife. One of the lessons you will have to learn quickly in this household is humility. And obedience. To God's will. In this house, I decide what is God's will."

"I understand."

"No, I don't think you do understand. You were snooping in my office. And just now, you were asking for a special favor. A proper wife would never do either of those things. You see," – and at this point he smiled again, now seemingly with the benevolence of a doting father – "we have to do God's will *all the time*, in all our words, and deeds, and even in our thoughts."

"I will try to do so." Renee tried to swallow back any other thoughts.

Ezekial dropped his patronizing smile and spoke in a level, serious tone. "One time, I was required to subject one of my wives to Penance. I really, honestly hated to do that. But God's will must be done at all times. I really hope you understand."

Chapter 14

The music was deafening, the carcasses were coming at her steadily, the blood was spattering her helmet and raincoat. Ruth learned to keep her feet on the grid because the floors were so slippery. Within an hour, her arms were trembling from the strain. On her second day at United Processing, she lasted an hour and a half before her strength gave out. Because she insisted on it, they let her stay on the line those days, even after she practically collapsed. Damien had told his father she needed a job desperately, and he had guaranteed she'd work out better than any of those women contract workers hired from Ezekial's religious corporation. Damien's father had hired Ruth almost as a joke, just to show his son he didn't know what he was talking about.

Amy's mother had sold her truck to Damien on paper so it would be even less likely to be tracked by Conception Control. Amy taught Ruth how to drive, and Ruth rode it to work at the United Processing plant in Neola County every day. The chances that Renee herself would come to work there were small, but the plan was to gather as much intelligence as possible about how Ezekial was operating.

John Leonides, whom everybody called "the Greek," supervised the boning room. He ranked only two steps higher than the clod pullers, but he ran the room with such efficiency and good humor that all the workers on the floor respected him. He wouldn't let her carry her gun anywhere on the floor; but she had learned to slice apart these giant mammals in seconds with her knife, and she didn't feel she needed an additional weapon in there. Ruth had told him of her farm experience and insisted on the hardest job. Because she was really productive for a beginner, and because of her diligent, no-nonsense attitude, the Greek left her alone when, on break, she sometimes left the boning room and chatted up the women contract workers elsewhere in the plant.

Like all employers everywhere, United Processing gave the least desirable jobs to its contract workers. Cleaning the lines of blood and grease, carting away and emptying barrels of offal, hand-carting boxes of packed product through the maze of passageways to the freezer, stacking the freezer, loading the trucks. A few of the women with office experience were given office jobs, but the regular office workers, afraid for their own jobs, made sure the manager knew every mistake those contract women made.

The contract women kept to themselves in their free time. Ruth ignored their hesitancy and tried to bond with them as a fellow new woman worker. She had cut her red pixie hair really short and covered it with a longer black wig which itself was barely visible under the bottom edge of her hard hat. She pretended she was rougher and slower than she was. She wanted them to think there was no harm in sharing information with this dumb clod puller.

The contract women brought their lunch in paper bags and hung out just outside the office door under the shade of a rusting corrugated steel roof. They had a beautiful view of the parking lot, which was surrounded on three sides by different parts of the plant. Ruth walked out of the processing room door and across the lot, pulling off her safety glasses and gloves, untying her blood-spattered raincoat and swinging it over her shoulder.

"At least it's cool where you work," one of the women offered.

"Hi. I'm Ruth. What's your name?"

"Naomi."

"Hi, Naomi." She looked at the others with what she hoped looked like a dopey grin. "What are your guys' names?"

"Abigail."

"Hi, Abigail."

"Ziba."

"Hi, Ziba."

"Azuban."

"Hi, um, Azuban."

"Ahinhoam."

"Wait a minute! You're playin' with me, right? These aren't your real names."

"These are the new names that have been given to us by our husbands. We're not allowed to use our old names."

Naomi seemed almost proud to take over as spokesperson for the group. She had dark hair tied up in two plaits. It looked like a new do, as the plaits weren't long enough to hang down gracefully yet. She had deep brown eyes. She looked like she was in her late twenties. Most of the women were in their late teens or early twenties.

"I won't be telling anybody. C'mon, what's your real name?"

Naomi looked at the other women, who were looking down or away. Naomi herself looked around before she confessed. "I'll tell you mine. I'm Sheila." Sheila looked at the others, but none of them spoke, so Ruth opened her own sandwich bag and started a conversation just with Sheila. Telling her real name seemed such as relief to Sheila that the rest of her story rushed out of her totally uncensored. Her last name was Manson. She used to live with her parents and her five-year-old boy. She had just found a steady job and was in the process of moving out when she was abducted by some motorcycle guys and taken to Ezekial, who had assigned her to a man in his congregation. She was his second wife, but they were fixing up a room in his house for a third. The first wife had been mean to her at first. The first wife was now coming around, but Sheila was afraid her son would grow up confused about who was his mother.

The other women were obviously listening intently. Sheila didn't mention the full name of her husband or the address where she lived, but Ruth didn't want to push too hard for information on the first day. Ruth told her she was an orphan, living with an uncle and an aunt in Cosgrove. She said they were okay as foster parents, but she took this job because she wanted to get out of the house as soon as possible, and it was the highest paying job she could find. Making up stories was not Ruth's strong point, so she hoped the women didn't ask too many detailed questions about her life.

These women's previous identities had been totally erased. The other women had seemed really shocked when Sheila reached out and told Ruth her real name. Ruth guessed they were bursting to tell their own stories. She hoped she would know everything about them by the end of the week. It would be none too soon.

* * * * * *

Don had been a machinist for many years until he hurt himself on the job. He was prescribed painkillers, and more painkillers, until he followed his new god, Oxycodone, right to heroin street, then out of his job and out of the family. By the time he recovered many years later, few employers were hiring machinists any more. His wife wouldn't let him move back into the house, so he started coming around secretly at night to see his children. Although he was branded, he had escaped from his latest addict detention facility, which had burned down shortly thereafter anyway. And he had a lot of spare time, and a lot of mechanical and electronic skills. He had built a blacked-out, battery-powered stealth motorcycle that could not be tracked – or even seen – at night. He had made a small killing selling the faux ankle bracelets that many of the teenagers of Kansas wore to show their contempt for the repressive regime.

According to the plan they had developed in Damien's record store that first night, Don was working to track all the Genesis Riders. He began following them at night with his stealth cycle to find out where they lived. But new Riders were signing up every day, attracted to the excitement of terrorizing and extorting money from citizens, and with the added benefit of forcing themselves on any eligible young woman they could capture. Don realized he could never keep up by tracking them to their homes one by one. So, one night he drove to Topeka and defeated the security measures and broke into Johnny's Motorcycle World and copied all their sales and service records. The next night he hit Bob's Big Barn O' Cycles in Kansas City.

"But all I came up with is the names and addresses of 63 male motorcycle owners in Neola County," he told Ruth glumly. They were meeting in Damien's darkened record store two weeks after the first meeting. Amy wasn't there. "I can't even tell which ones are Riders."

Since there were no official records of which women had been abducted and where they were kept, they were just trying to get whatever information they could. Ruth had gotten the real name and former address of just one woman at United Processing, Sheila, but even Sheila didn't know her own current address. Don had nothing but the 63 addresses. Damien didn't have any information about the Riders or the women. He did report that United Processing was very happy with Ruth's work, and his father had admitted he had been wrong about her. Apparently, the word among the men at the plant was not to mess with that new girl.

"We're getting nowhere," Don sighed. "Should we try the courts again?"

"There's already a court order out there telling the sheriff to stop letting them do it." Ruth face was grim. "It hasn't done any good. Do we have to kidnap Ezekial?"

"No! I'm against that. That would turn him into a victim in the eyes of the law."

"You guys need to know," Damien interrupted, "the guys actually taking the women are not keeping their names a secret." They looked at him. He winced like he was sorry he said that, but then he went ahead. "They come in here sometimes. They don't even notice me. I hear them bragging all the time."

"Do you have a list of their names?"

"Nicknames. A few. Their leader is called Hunter."

"What about real names? From their credit cards or sales receipts?"

"They usually use cash."

"But you can ask their real names and addresses, can't you?"

"Are you trying to get me killed?"

Chapter 15

Renee had overnight baby duty but was expected to be up and ready to go by seven. There was an infant, an eight month old and a one year old. No one told her their names. They had a pretty quiet night. She enjoyed watching them sleep, imagining her own child at each of these ages. She didn't know the sex of her child, and Kansas law forbade any investigations into the sex or condition of the fetus.

The house wasn't designed for a sixth wife, and so she had to double up with another wife. Dina appeared in the nursery to bring her to her room. Renee knew she had to hide the joy in her heart when she saw Moira, her friend from when they were first captured and held in the Rider's clubhouse.

"So great to see you!" she whispered once Dina was out of the room. Moira, still half asleep, sat up on her bed groggily, but she smiled. They hugged like lifelong friends. She guessed Moira had been sold by the Riders, then taken back, just as she had been.

"Are they taking all the women here now?"

"Are you kidding? There's hundreds of women. This is Bible Land, Ezekial's own place. It's brand new. We're his personal wives. The rest are scattered all over the county."

"Moira, I …."

Moira put a finger to Renee's lips. "Don't ever say that name here. We're all given new biblical names. My name here is Mara. I lucked out getting a name close to my real name." She paused, looking meaningfully at Renee. "Well, I guess it wasn't really luck."

"What do you mean?"

"He likes me. And I know how to keep him liking me. A lot."

"Oh, *Mara*, that doesn't sound right."

"You'll see. Sooner or later, you'll wish you could do anything, *anything*, to have him say a kind word to you."

Renee's night had been made easier by Dina, who appeared every hour or so and helped change the babies' diapers if they needed changing. Renee had tried to talk to her, but Dina just smiled and nodded her head and went about doing the dirtiest parts of the job. She seemed friendly enough, but Renee wondered if she was deaf. Then she appeared again in the doorway of the bedroom in the middle of Renee's conversation with Mara. Mara waved her in, and Dina pointed to Renee's bed, which had just been placed in the room a few minutes before. "Clean sheets," she said, and Mara nodded. Before Renee could ask her about this, she heard a soft bell sound, almost like a doorbell, and the woman ran out of the room.

"That's the breakfast bell," Mara told her. "Dina serves. The whole family eats together. We all have to be there."

There was a long kitchen table that could seat at least ten, but there was also an adjoining room that was a little smaller and had French doors that led to the back yard. Reverend Ezekial sat in this smaller room with his back to the yard. There were three places set on the table in that room besides his. Renee was called into that room and motioned to sit down. At the other end of the table from Ezekial was Joan. Her casual but chic light blue dress and her styled light brown hair and simple silver earrings signaled her status as first wife. She looked like she was a well-preserved forty. Renee wondered if this was going to be another Mrs. Prescott experience. But maybe being one of multiple wives had been new to Mrs. Prescott. Maybe Joan was used to being just one of many wives by now.

She seemed to use them as servants. Renee sat down across from a different wife she had never seen before. Her voluptuous features could be detected even under her Puritan costume, her blonde braids were thick and long, but her face was pudgy and her skin bad. Renee wondered how much makeup and cleanser they would be allowed. She did figure Ezekial wanted them to look at least halfway decent. The blonde wife nodded to her but did not say anything. The places were already set with plain white china. Dina and Mara rushed in and out with dishes of sausage and eggs, pancakes, bacon, juices, a coffeepot. Renee could hear the table being set in the next room, and over the shoulder of the blonde she could see Dina again, serving the others.

Ezekial announced they would all stop while they said grace. Starting with Joan, he asked each wife, both around his table and the table in the next room, to compose a prayer. Renee was used to saying grace like this, and whatever she said didn't seem to cause anyone's eyebrows to be raised. She was afraid Ezekial would launch into a long-winded stemwinder, but he seemed as hungry as anybody. Ezekial told the two other wives at the table to introduce themselves. Deborah, the woman with the blonde braids, forced a smile and nodded. Renee wondered if an added wife was a plus or a minus to a present wife like Deborah.

"Hello, and welcome to our happy family." Joan, the original wife, spoke without an audible trace of irony. "I am Joan, First Wife."

"Hello, my name is Renee."

"No, it's not," Ezekial interrupted. He took the rest of the piece of bacon he was chewing on and held it like a pointer. "That's your old, secular name. Everyone in this household gets a new name." He turned to the other wives. "I already told her, her new name is Tamar. Explain this to her, Joan."

As Joan turned to her, a silver earring flashed in the morning sunlight. "You are in the service of God now. You must reject your past sinful life." Joan spoke in such a monotone Renee imagined this was a memorized spiel. "You will be retrained and disciplined here to understand and carry out God's will. Your child will be raised in the ways of godliness by our family. And God willing, you will bring forth more children."

"Who will be the father of these 'more children?'"

The other two wives froze, and a dead silence came over the room. Even Ezekial stopped eating and dropped his hands to the table. Ezekial glared at Joan.

"Your husband, of course," Joan responded.

"What if I don't want to have a child with him?"

"You don't have a choice, dear." And now Joan did seem to be enjoying herself a little. It looked like Joan was taking some satisfaction in the prospect of seeing yet another woman about to be degraded to a status below her own. The other wife was staring at Renee.

"What if I don't let him do it?"

Joan turned to Ezekial. "Are these the kind of things we should talk about at the breakfast table? I am seeking your guidance here." Ezekial motioned with his fingers for her to go on. Joan nodded, her mouth now downturned, sour.

"If it comes down to that, we could force you. But we don't like physical violence in God's household." Joan, with her light, fluffy, styled hair, and her silver earrings, and her chic light blue dress, did not look eager to engage in violence. "Instead, we've set up a Place of Penance for this family, and all the families of God, to send recalcitrant wives. If you refuse, you will be sent there, to be dealt with by those who know how to change behavior." Joan was now staring at Renee. "No one who has been sent to the Place of Penance has ever been disobedient again."

✳ ✳ ✳   ✳ ✳ ✳

Renee snuck out of overnight nursery duty to visit Mara in their room. When Mara looked up in surprise, Renee quickly hushed her. "Don't worry. Dina is covering for me." Mara sat up in her bed, barely visible in the light that came from the hallway through the small glass pane in the door. Renee continued in a voice little more than a whisper. "What's with that girl, Dina? I'm just a new slave here, but even I can push her around."

Mara sat up. "Do you like your new name?"

"Tamar? I guess it's okay. I never heard of Tamar before. I can't see why he didn't let me keep Renee."

"You were smart not to argue."

"Yeah. Things were getting a little frosty in there. I mean, even First Wifey was looking a little tense."

"I don't mean just that. You might have been sent to Penance just for arguing. That's what happened to Dina. She made fun of the way things are here."

"Dina? I can't imagine her making fun of anything. She's such a humble slave."

"She is now. Ever since she came back from Penance."

Renee slumped down on the bed next to Mara. She had an urge to put an arm around her. She needed to feel close to somebody. But it was too risky, in too many ways.

"What if Ezekial comes for me tonight?"

"You don't have any choice. It won't be your fault."

She sobbed. Then Mara put an arm around her. Then she really cried, bawled. "I just want to raise my own kid," she finally managed.

"I can imagine. But at least Ezekial won't be his real father. When I get pregnant next time, I will know Ezekial is the father. He'll actually have legal rights and everything. I don't know if I can bear that."

Chapter 16

The Law Enforcement Committee voted to approve Stacey's anti-branding bill. The vote was 22-16, with six of the majority votes coming from CP members. The bill was taken to the House floor, where it was given precedence over a number of other bills and was quickly passed by a majority vote. The Senate took up the bill almost immediately and passed it. Then Governor Adams signed it quickly, admitting that her earlier signing of the branding bill had been a mistake.

Martha stood in the doorway to Stacey's office with her hands on her hips. "You are good, Stacey Davenport. You are really good. It is an honor to work with such an example of a supremely empowered woman. I mean that."

Martha's face was suffused with admiration as she stepped forward into Stacey's hug. Stacey had felt embattled and alone ever since she came to Topeka. She knew who her allies were, but she had no real friends in the legislature. She had told herself this was necessary because she had so many secrets to hide. She suddenly realized she was holding on to Martha's hug a little too long. She didn't like being in Topeka totally without actual friends.

"I have a sort of ... *understanding* with someone very powerful. It's got nothing to do with politics, really. It's a personal thing."

Martha leaned back out of the hug and looked at her. "Golsch, of course. Stacey, I really, really hope it isn't ...."

"Hold on." Stacey's choices were stark. Remain a mysterious and cold *political operative* whom Martha could only admire from a distance, or let Martha in on the things that were bothering her. She hugged Martha again, briefly. "Can you sit down?"

"It's all but certain," Stacey began, "that Roland's father

is Robert Golsch."

"Oh my God! Golsch? Roland's father is Golsch? Was he that man at the funeral?"

Stacey nodded. "He blames me for leading his son down the wrong path."

Martha held up her hand to stop her, taking a deep breath, then pushing her blue-framed glasses back onto her flushed face.

"Let me make a confession right now. I do too, Stacey. I blame you. I can't help it. He was a really, really good friend of mine."

"I can tell you were in love with him," Stacey blurted out. She didn't let Martha respond. "I was in love with him, too. And I knew something you didn't. All the time he was fighting for the Independent Party ideals, he was fighting against his own father."

"Golsch. Oh."

"I thought he was really brave, as brave as a man could be in his position. I thought I could help him."

Martha slumped down in the chair next to Stacey's desk. "I thought I was helping him, too. Until you came along." She fluttered her hand helplessly, then laid it down on the desk in a gesture of defeat.

Stacey put her hand over Martha's. "Is there any point in fighting over him now? He was more complicated than either of us imagined."

Martha sat up straighter. She seemed to recover her composure. "I'm a realist, Stacey. I should have known Roland had a secret side. I guess everybody has a secret side." She withdrew her hand and scrutinized Stacey's face as if she were trying to discover Stacey's secret side.

"I can tell you this much. Golsch has a connection with me. It's complicated. It's personal. It's not political."

"Of course. You were engaged to his son!"

"Golsch encouraged me to put in the anti-branding bill. Of course, you figured out he's the one who got the bill passed."

Stacey had to stop herself. She had told the truth, but not all of it. The other half was that Golsch himself was an addict, and he had a real, personal self-interest in repealing the branding bill. But Stacey wasn't going to reveal this part of it to Martha. She didn't have the heart to reveal this personal weakness of Golsch, a weakness she had discovered only because she was an addict herself. And addicts had to stick together.

Chapter 17

The previous summer, Grant had taken all his vacation time and flown out to Kansas seven times to try to help Stacey's political campaign. But, while in Kansas, he had learned she had definitely moved on. She had even gotten engaged to Roland, even humiliated herself in front of the whole state by agreeing to be his second wife. Grant had decided he was sick of it and made a hard exit on election night. When she tried to call him a few weeks later, he had refused to pick up.

But she called again a few weeks after he started with Eleni.

"Grant, I know you're busy back there in Boston. But can you talk to me for just a minute?"

"… um…yeah."

"You sound busy. What are you doing right now, exactly?"

"Eleni and I just came in from dinner. She forgot her pocketbook and went back to the car to get it."

"Oh. This is not a good time. I'll call you some other time."

"No, you might as well keep talking. Even if you hang up right now, I have to tell her about it."

"What?"

"Massachusetts law. Anyone in a sexual relationship must report any contact with a previous sex partner to the current partner within 72 hours of the contact." He rattled off the requirement of the law like the lawyer he was.

"A sexual relationship?"

"I have to tell you that, too, if you ask. So, I guess I've told you that. I didn't expect it, me and Eleni, to happen so soon, but there it is."

"You have 72 hours?"

"I'm telling her immediately. What did you want to talk about? Hey, I forgot to congratulate you. Great victory in the MOMS fight! You already seem to have the Certainty Party on the run! I can't imagine anyone else but you accomplishing that. You should be really proud."

"Thanks, Grant. Things are a little better now. But Ruth's sister, Renee, is still captured."

"I don't understand Kansas. You've got a federal court order to stop those abductions."

"You know Reverend Ezekial ignores that order."

"Please tell me you won't ever set foot in his county."

"I'll do what I have to do." There was a long silence on the line. It wasn't because of her snippy answer. It was because Grant was waiting for her to say why she had called him.

She told him why. "Grant, it was as much my fault as yours. I called just to ask you not to hate me."

*** ***

Grant duly notified Eleni, as required by Massachusetts law, that he had engaged in verbal contact with a partner with whom he had previously had a sexual relationship. The results were not good.

"You still love her, don't you?" she accused him. They were recovering on the table in the locked office at lunch time. He had put off telling her about the phone call with Eleni for 64 hours, almost the legal limit.

"No, I do not. I admire her courage to even live in that state. But millions of people do, I guess."

"You definitely do admire her. She's a hero to you, isn't she?"

"No, I ...." He let his words trail off while he put his clothes on. She did the same.

"Maybe a political hero," he admitted.

"I don't want to hear it," she sniffed.

"Eleni, let me tell you this much. She is deeply, deeply compromised. On a personal level. And she hurt me. I don't want to be hurt like that again."

*** ***

Eleni was late for their planned dinner a few weeks later. "Where have you been?"

"To the doctor. I just have a cold," Eleni explained.

He didn't believe her. She didn't have a cold. Why would she lie to him? For the next several days, he observed her closely. No cold. No nothing. It was a misdemeanor in Massachusetts to coerce or pressure anyone to reveal their reason for a doctor's visit, so he couldn't push the issue. But she noticed he was glum.

"What's wrong?" she asked. "It's Stacey, isn't it? You miss being in Kansas, fighting on her side."

"No, I'm done with her. I do miss the fight in Kansas; but, believe me, I wouldn't be much help in that fight. They were making fun of me by the end. Honestly, my feeling is, it would be nice if I could return her calls. But not nice enough to risk losing you."

"Grant, if that's going to make you like, permanently sad, maybe you really should re-think things between us."

"I'm *not* pining for her! I'm just thinking about *us*."

"Well, if you're thinking about us, what about us is making you so moody these days?"

He sighed, and his voice came out deeper. "The doctor. Why did you go to the doctor?"

"That question's not allowed." Her voice was tiny.

"I know it's not allowed. But I feel like I have some kind of a right to know."

"Not any legal right." This was the response he expected. She was a law student, after all.

"Sure, I understand. I don't have any legal right to know. But I want to know. You had an abortion, right?"

She bristled. "Whether I had an abortion or not has nothing at all to do with you."

"Nothing? Oh, come on. Maybe legally, but ... aren't we more than just legal?"

"We're not even married. I think we're actually a little less than legal." But then she grimaced at her own facile wordplay. "Sorry. I didn't mean to downplay our relationship. You're right. It is more than legal." She met his eyes. "I want your trust, Grant. Yes, I had an abortion."

Chapter 18

Ruth, Amy and Don met in Damien's record store again the following week to share intelligence. They agreed that all their meetings would be after dark, when they could more safely travel, and after the store had closed.

Ruth stopped there on her way home from work and hung out in back until the others arrived. Damien was still intimidated by her. He didn't mind the slaughterhouse smell she carried on her clothes after work. It reminded him of his father, the plant manager, coming home years earlier, long after dark, with that same odor. But Damien generally avoided talking to Ruth until after Don appeared.

"They have a clubhouse." Damien reported on his eavesdropping on the Genesis Riders, who had been bragging in the record store the previous week. "It's a barn behind a deserted old farmhouse. Sounds like it's down a long driveway off Rover Mill Road. That's where they take the women first before they turn them over to Reverend Ezekial."

Ruth didn't bother to hide her annoyance at Damien for waiting until after dark to reveal this information. "How long do they keep them there before they ship them off to Ezekial," she snapped. "Could my sister still be in that clubhouse?"

"They only keep them there until they get fresh replacements. Sounds like nobody stays there for long."

"I wonder if anybody there keeps records of where the women go after that," Don speculated.

Damien smirked. "You don't know these guys. They were arguing yesterday over how much they got paid for some woman. They couldn't remember. They almost got into a fight. Nobody keeps records. Nobody writes anything down about anything, I'm sure."

"I'll go there tonight anyway and bug every motorcycle

that shows."

"I'm not finished." Damien surprised all of them by interrupting. "There's another place they go. It sounds like they bring some of the women back to this place for just a few days sometimes. For punishment. They call the place Penance. It's near the clubhouse."

"So, Renee could be sent there, too." Ruth grimaced.

Damien shook his head. "Not likely. These guys were laughing. They said Hunter must be doing too good a job of punishment, because less and less women are being sent there all the time."

"I'll scout out Penance, too." Don seemed excited.

"What good will that do?" Ruth complained. "What we need to know is, *where are the women being held?*"

Don shrugged. "This won't help us find the women; but when we do find the women, any information we have will help us get them out." He pulled Ruth to him, put his arm around her shoulders even as she stiffened. "I know it's frustrating, honey. I know you want to use that gun. But we need intelligence first. We'll get it one piece at a time."

*** ***

Ruth stepped up her spying and prying during her breaks at United Processing. She tried to josh and joke the women into giving up their real names. They seemed very reluctant. Ziba in particular was having none of it.

"Stop! Stop!" she talked over another woman who had started to give Ruth her real name. "This is unholy! Our secular names were given to us by the devil. Reverend Ezekial has blessed us with a second chance to live in God's grace, but only if only we obey."

"I should be able to say my real name," one of the contract women spoke up. "It's the name I was baptized with. Why can't I say it?"

"Because you're going to end up in Penance." Ziba was almost in tears. "Nobody they send to Penance ever comes back the same."

All the other women seemed shocked into silence. The official word from Ezekial was that the renaming system was designed to emphasize that the fallen women needed new identities for their new, now-blessed lives. But Ruth could easily see that the renaming had another purpose. It made these women untraceable to their families, friends, and law enforcement. No one, not even their sister wives, could help any outsider find any particular woman who had been taken.

Ruth realized that some of the women were so indoctrinated already they could not be trusted. Her plan had been to set up a little spy ring that could locate where all the taken women were located. She was shocked that Ziba didn't even seem to want to be rescued. She remembered well the time she had spent chained to an iron ring in the cabana behind Ezekial's old house. She would be risking her own freedom now if she continued to try pushing the whole group toward resistance.

Early the next morning, she started on a new plan. The contract women's van always arrived almost half an hour before the plant was officially open. Ruth arrived early too, and she went right to the boning room and turned on the lights. She put on her yellow slicker, plastic helmet and yellow hood designed to keep most of the blood splatter off of her clothes. She then went out to the women, who were outside, standing or resting against barrels or hulks of broken-down machinery near their lunch place. It was still cool enough outside; they didn't need to stand in the shade. She said hi to all of them, nodding in her intentionally dopey way. Then she asked Sheila if she would help her clear some spilled remains that had made their way to the boning room floor.

"Sure."

"Shoulda been cleaned up yesterday." Ruth pretended to be annoyed.

But, once inside, Ruth led Sheila right past the boning room to the door to the chiller. She grabbed the heavy metal handle and pulled open the door. The lights were on as if it were normal starting time, but no one was there except she and Sheila. Ruth had her gun under her slicker; her truck was backed to the curb in the parking lot in case she had to make a quick exit. She pulled Sheila quickly into the chiller. She closed the door, turned around. She had to trust somebody.

Ruth forced herself to talk quietly, and in her normal tone of voice. "I'm trusting you with my freedom, and I'm offering you yours."

Sheila's eyes widened in surprise. "What do you mean?"

"I'm not just a clod puller. There is a movement of people who are resisting the enslavement of women in this county. They're willing to take big risks to free those who want to be free."

Sheila still acted stunned. "But it's the law, right?"

"No. They want you to believe that, but it's not. What they're doing is illegal, though the sheriff won't stop them. The only question is, do you want to be free?"

Sheila's eyes drifted up to the flickering circular light in the ceiling as if receiving a communication from heaven. "Oh, yes. Yes. Before my little Bobby starts calling my new husband Daddy."

"You can help the resistance movement. We're trying to collect the real names of as many of the women as we can, and the addresses where they're being held captive. If you could just get me that information, that would be a huge help."

"Isn't there a list?" Sheila asked.

"Not that we know of."

"You'd better work quick. I'm sure Ziba is going to tell her husband you're asking about their real names."

"Is her husband Ezekial?"

"No."

"So, maybe he's a nobody, and they won't really care that much about what he says."

Sheila shrugged her shoulders slightly. "I'll do anything to get us out of here."

"Could you get me the list the van driver uses to figure out where to pick up the contract women?"

"Yeah. Maybe. I think so."

"Good. Listen. One more thing. When we come to get you, you won't have any notice. You'll have to trust us. It will be a man or a girl. They each have marks on their faces, like this." Ruth drew a finger down the center of her forehead.

"Oh. You mean markos."

"Yes. Or it could be me." Ruth pulled back her plastic hood, grabbed at her hair, unpinned the wig, and exposed her matted, thick, natural red hair.

Sheila's eyes grew huge. Her mouth dropped open.

Ruth was offended. "I didn't think I looked *that* bad."

"No. No. No. It's just … I've seen you before!"

The door to the chiller suddenly opened with a refrigerator-door squishing sound. The two women froze. It was too late to turn out the light. They could hear footsteps treading the metal grills on the floor. Ruth's hands trembled as she tried to put her black wig back on. Sheila reached up to try to help straighten it. Then a strong arm suddenly pushed a carcass aside right in front of them. And they were staring into her boss's dark brown eyes.

"Hey, ladies! I hope I'm not interrupting anything." John Leonides, the Greek, was too smart not to be suspicious. But he didn't act suspicious.

"We were just, uh, talking about a recipe."

"A secret recipe, huh? So secret you had to come in here early and close the door." John was not stupid. "A recipe for what? I'm quite a big cook myself." His playing along with their ruse was unnerving. John was stocky but very short. Ruth was calculating how quickly she could get her gun out from under her slicker. Her knife was easier to reach. He glanced at her wig. She could feel it wasn't on straight.

"Kale pie," Sheila practically shouted, drawing his attention back toward her. "Like spinach pie, only with kale."

John drew back. "Ew! That'll make you sick for sure!" Then his expression turned somber. He looked quietly from one to the other. "What's going on?"

"I need to go back outside. My shift has already started." Sheila didn't work directly for John.

"Yeah, you better do that, hon." John's tone was indecipherable to Ruth. He turned to Ruth as soon as Sheila was gone.

"You have something to do with those contract girls Reverend Ezekial sends over here, don't you?" His face was open and his voice so friendly and relaxed she started to loosen her grip on the knife, but she reminded herself not to fall for this. "I see you've been wearing fake hair," he added.

Ruth tightened her hold on the knife. She figured she had nothing to lose. If she had to kill him, she'd have to do it fast before the other workers got there. But there was something about his relaxed, almost fatherly gaze that told her she might not have to worry. At some point, you have to trust somebody, she reminded herself.

"I used to be one of those captured women. I escaped."

His mouth dropped open as his dark eyes peered into hers. "My daughter tried to tell me about that capturing women stuff. I thought she was making it up. But it's true?"

"Your daughter wasn't making it up. All those contract women who work here. They were taken as second or third wives against their will. They're basically slaves."

John put his hand to his face, fingers spread in shock.

"Oh, my. Does the company know about this?"

"John, I don't know. But the worst thing you can do is bring it up. There's like, a resistance movement. Some of these contract women are helping us. It's important they keep coming here."

"Oh. I guess I should pay more attention to what's going on." She assured him her story was true, and more than a hundred women had already been taken. A pained expression came over his face. "My daughter …. This is awful." He stood staring at the hanging carcasses. Then he suddenly snapped to attention. "I gotta go before the rest of the workers arrive." He turned to go – but then turned back suddenly and put his hands to her face. She gasped and held the knife tighter. But then, with a very gentle touch, he set her wig back on straight.

As soon as he was gone, she burst into tears.

An hour later, while she was working on the line, she saw him lurch out of his office in the rolling gait of a very short, very wide man. He joked with each man on the line, as was his habit. As he approached her, he put his index finger up as if they were in an argument and was about to refute something she had said. Ruth had a sudden fear that he had informed the company about her. He came close and leaned in toward her.

"About our talk this morning. You weren't serious about what you said, right?"

She braced herself.

"There's no such thing as kale pie, right?"

*** ***

When Ruth slouched toward the women in the yard at lunch time, she could see that Sheila was almost shaking with repressed excitement. Now that she had Sheila as an inside source of information, Ruth no longer had to ask the other women for their real names. She put on an especially dopey act that afternoon, trying to impress Ziba with how stupid and harmless she was – nobody worth telling her husband about. But underneath she was dying to hear what Sheila had found out for her.

Sitting on opposite sides of the bench under the tin roof, they managed to linger until after the other women had started walking back.

"I told John the truth," Ruth started. "He's a good guy. I think we're okay with him."

"Oh, thank God! I've been waiting to be dragged away all morning."

"I'm sure he's not telling anyone. Did you get the list from the van?" Ruth was talking fast. Anyone walking outside the building could see them.

"No. But listen. When I saw you without your wig, I knew I'd seen you somewhere before."

"I was on television a couple of times during Stacey's campaign. That's probably where you saw me."

"We're not allowed to watch television. Hey, you were captured once, right?"

"Right."

"That's it! I remember now. I saw you once at Ezekial's house in Bible Land."

"I've never been to Bible Land."

Ruth was annoyed. She wanted Sheila to come up with a plan to get those names and addresses from the van. They only had a few seconds to talk alone before people would notice. And it really didn't make any difference whether they had seen each other before or not. Unless ....

"I know it was you," Sheila insisted. "Or somebody who looks almost exactly like you. With that red hair. Like a twin sister or something."

Chapter 19

Stacey had never realized before that there were two sets of people in whatever state you lived in. There were the people with regular jobs and health insurance and a regular place to stay – and then there were people like her.

All through college and law school, she had kept an emotional distance from her family. She also had avoided the many reminders of her drug-addicted past in Cosgrove. After her father decided he loved Oxycontin more than his family, she watched her mother frantically hold the rest of the family together. But Stacey couldn't stand her mother's hysteria, or the relentless chaos it caused. For all those years Stacey had kept her family at a distance, but she always had a plan for helping them. She would become a wealthy and powerful lawyer. Then she would help them all she could – from a distance.

Her campaign had changed all of that. She'd gotten to know her little brother Kendrick again. She had bonded with her little sister, Amy. Amy showed her the brand on her forehead. Stacey confessed some of the sordid things she'd done as an addict. She'd watched her mother swing into action once she was shown a way to fight the Certainty Party. She'd found out her father had not only recovered from his addiction but had even regained his old spirit and sense of ingenuity and fun.

She hadn't seen her father since election night, but she knew Amy had now found him. He was part of their underground resistance now. She could feel in her heart he was near, but she wished he was there in person to talk to.

Her token salary as a Kansas state delegate paid her personal expenses and for her cut-rate visits to the doctor Martha had recommended. If she had to pay rent, she wouldn't even break even. She had to stay in the legislature to help the Independents hold off the misogynous bills still being passed by the Certainty Party. She couldn't get a legal job because the Professional Reform Act barred all pregnant women and women with children from graduating from law school. She needed a job, and it would have to come with health care benefits because of the giant hospital bill that was coming when she gave birth to her child. And after the birth, what would happen then?

But finances were the least of her worries. The Certainty Party had already put in a new bill, called MOMS-2, that they were promoting as a kinder, gentler version of MOMS. Under MOMS-2, women whose children were conceived out of wedlock would not have to be taken as concubines by a married man of religion – but their children would be taken from them and raised in a clergy-sanctioned household.

Everyone knew Governor Adams would veto it, so the issue, again, was whether the CP could get a veto-proof two-thirds majority vote to override the veto. Martha made it clear that the Independents were expecting her to lead the charge against the bill. Stacey could not afford to quit the legislature – but she could not afford to stay.

She had an obligation to her unborn child. She steeled herself to make the necessary call to Grant. She caught him at his apartment when Eleni wasn't there. "You told me a while ago you wanted to be involved in raising our daughter. Do you still feel that way, Grant?"

"There's no daughter yet. There's not even any baby," he snapped back.

His tone deflated any secret hopes she might have had. She would have to keep re-learning what it felt like to humble herself. She used to be so proud. After Grant had momentarily panicked and run away when she had first told him she was pregnant, she had ignored all his pleas for forgiveness. But after she started her affair with Roland, his begging stopped. He didn't want any part of her. She had to take that. But she also had to keep on going.

"Um, I didn't want to say this, but I could go to court for support."

"It wouldn't work. Don't you keep up on the law? The Supreme Court has ruled that one state can refuse to enforce the judgments of another state on any matter that first state deems to be a religious matter. That includes all domestic and support judgments. You can't get financial support out of me that way."

"Why are you being so mean?" This conversation was going worse than she'd ever imagined. Suddenly she was sobbing.

"You know I'm not cheap, Stacey." He sounded chastened. "I'll pay you whatever you need."

"Thank you." But she hardly felt any better. "Don't you want to be a father, too?" This just slipped out. Even to her, her voice sounded thin, far away, like she had already given up and was just going through the motions. "You wouldn't have to interact with me at all. We could make some kind of arrangements. You could even bring Eleni to Kansas when you come to see the baby. I'll keep out of your way."

"Please don't beg. This doesn't sound like the Stacey I used to know."

Chapter 20

Most of the wives sat together later that morning to watch Ezekial's televised Sunday service. It was the only show the wives were permitted to watch. Ezekial no longer displayed all of his wives on television. There was too much risk that their relatives would see and identify them. Ezekial brought only Joan, who sat in the first pew, and one other wife, who was forced to wear a veil during the televised portion of the service. As the rest of the wives assembled in Bible Land to watch the service, Mara gave Renee instructions on how to act.

"Don't think you can get away with just bowing your head reverently the whole time. You have to look up, look interested, laugh at his jokes, or at least smile."

"Who's to know? He can't see us through the television."

"The other wives know. The children are trained to watch you. Don't make the mistake Dina made. Dina was smirking, she was mocking him. She really was funny. One of the kids tattled on her. You see how terrified of everything she is now. She's a complete slave, even to us."

"She was a regular person before …?"

"Yep."

The ceremony was shown on an 88-inch television screen in the family room. Ezekial stood at the pulpit in the front of his enormous church. There was a rustling of people being seated as if they had been standing or singing hymns. The first thing viewers saw was a zoom-in to a close-up of the preacher. Renee looked at Mara, who was sitting beside her in the family room. Mara braved a little smirk.

Joan, the first wife, was required to attend the service in person, so Dina had been left in charge of the other wives and the children. She didn't seem to have any organizational skills or any plan, but this made it even more difficult for Renee, who constantly had to guess what she was supposed to do at any given point of the proceedings. She decided to do whatever Mara did.

On the screen, Ezekial began in a voice so soft it was almost inaudible. He told a story of a family, a man, a wife and two children. Speaking almost in a whisper, he told how Satan tempted the children into evil, tempted their mother to stray, tempted the father to drink. How the family was destroyed and they all were sucked down into eternal damnation. "We humans are not able to resist, on our own, this powerful demon who would destroy our lives. He will destroy our lives. He will make sure we sin and are punished by eternal damnation. Burning in the flames of hell, forever. All of us.

"And why? Because we have disobeyed the will of Almighty God." His voice picked up volume. "But God is here to help us. He has sent his Son. He has sent his word in the Holy Bible. He has sent his messengers, his prophets, his holy clergymen. He has sent me." Suddenly he was shouting. "He has sent *me*. Yes, I am God's ordained holy messenger. He has revealed to me that Satan's minions are all among us in this country, and even in this state. And God has directed me to destroy them!

"All I'm asking of you is to let me loose. Help me help God destroy the Satanists among us. They march under all kinds of banners." He almost spat out the names. "Atheists, agnostics, secularists, humanists – all just fancy words for deniers of the true word of God. And those words are revealed in the Holy Bible. People, it's a *book*. It tells us what to do. Just do it!"

Ezekial was breathing hard. He managed to say between breaths that he had been with God, spoken to God, and God told him the meaning of every word of the bible. God was apparently against any kind of government that Ezekial didn't control, against any kind of education that taught anything except his own exact interpretation of the bible.

"We must destroy the abominations that the secular state has imposed on His children. All children must be home schooled by trained and disciplined women to avoid this insidious indoctrination by the secularists." Ezekial continued his litany of commands that God had given him directly. Immunizations should be forbidden because they were an attempt to thwart the will of God. Wives should not work outside the home. All women were weak and should not be allowed outside the home at all except on an authorized errand or with a male relative. Women who were proven to be impure should be taken under the care of a male experienced in guiding women. God commanded all this, Ezekial claimed, and he had the biblical quotes to prove it. He waved his arms as he shouted quote after quote, most of which had never been spoken in any Christian church before. This went on for most of an hour. But even with all his enthusiasm, Ezekial seemed to flag by the end.

"God will prevail!" he suddenly shouted in a last burst of zeal. "We will prevail! We will smite the infidels, the secularists, and all the other minions of Satan. We will root them out of our government, our schools, our places of worship, even our own houses! Bow down to God! Bow down to God! Come forward and be blessed! Let me put the mark of God upon you."

Mara turned to Renee and raised her eyebrows slightly. Renee ventured a smile. On the screen, a long line of church members was coming slowly forward, one by one, to receive Ezekial's blessing. A voiceover asked for donations as biblical quotes about charity scrolled across the screen. First it was a deep professional announcer's voice, then various of Ezekial's acolytes, then male parishioners, then a woman parishioner. Finally, a child's voice begged for money. By this time, the biblical quotes on the screen had been replaced with explicit directions for how to send your money. The line of churchgoers waiting to be blessed went on longer than the recording, so the recorded donation voices were simply run by again. And again.

*** ***

"That woman is not happy."

Audrey had been watching Reverend Ezekial's church services with Amy the week before. She always watched so she could shout back at the TV, and also so she could see if Ezekial was still fulminating personally against Stacey, who had beat his candidate in the recent election. But the reverend hadn't been on Stacey's case for a few weeks now. Audrey's observation referred to Ezekial's first wife, Joan, who always sat in the first pew during Ezekial's Sunday sermons and was often shown on camera, trying to smile.

Her mother's words echoed in Amy's consciousness for a week. Her father had said they should collect any information – anything – about Ezekial's organization that they could find. Her mother had pretty good instincts for how people were feeling, so Amy filed away in her head this information that Ezekial's wife was unhappy. Anything could be important.

The conspirators decided to meet twice a week at night in Damien's record store. At the next meeting, Ruth came in late, spotted with blood and smelling of offal. Don asked her right away if she had gotten any information from United Processing.

"Not much," she answered simply. "The driver of the van picks up the contract workers every day. He's got to have a list in the van of where they live. I'm trying to get that."

"Okay, that's something. It's only addresses, but that's a start."

Ruth's face was closed off like she was holding something back. But she couldn't. "One of the women, who calls herself Ziba, is totally brainwashed. And she's suspicious. She says she's going to tell her husband I was asking the women their real names."

"We better pull you out of there."

Ruth shook her head. "No. Not yet."

"It's too dangerous."

"I can't leave now. I just found out something," Ruth insisted, turning to look out the window of the store at the empty road in front. There was a catch in her voice.

"Spit it out, Ruth." Amy was too tired to put up with any mysteries that night.

"Okay." Ruth's eyes lit up as she caught each of theirs. "My sister. I think I found my sister. Sheila saw me without my wig. She says she saw a woman who looks exactly like me. Renee has red hair, too. She does look exactly like me. It's her. She's a captive in Ezekial's own house. Not the place I was kept in. She's in his new house in Bible Land."

"Oh, great!" Amy dared to hug her. Don hugged the both of them. Even Damien tentatively joined in, his arms barely touching anybody. "We'll get her out. We'll get her."

"But I'm still going back to the processing plant. I owe Sheila. I promised I'd get her out, too."

* * * * * *

Amy and Don left a few minutes later for Bible Land. They rode on his stealth motorcycle, his blacked-out, off-the-grid, battery powered invention without any lights or reflectors, guided at night only by an infrared screen – a machine that he had built himself and successfully used for months to avoid detection by the police, Conception Control, and the Genesis Riders. Bible Land was in Neola County, fifteen miles west of Neola City, close to the end of his battery range. Amy put her arms around her father's waist and leaned into him. She had never been that deep into Neola County. A tiny spear of fear ran through her body as they progressed deeper into Ezekial's territory. She held her father tight and rested her head on his shoulder, trying to dissolve her fear in his warmth.

Amy took courage in the fact that her father was always riding somewhere out in this county every night. There were a lot of reasons why he shouldn't be there. He wasn't just an addict who was missing from his rehab facility. And he wasn't just the father of Stacey Davenport, archenemy of Ezekial and the Genesis Riders. He was also a suspect in the death of Roland. The whole justice system of Neola County was run by Ezekial and the Riders, and Don was probably risking his life by cruising at night right under their noses. But he never acted afraid.

The bright moonlight increased the danger but enhanced the beauty of the black and silvery landscape. Amy's little spearpoint of fear gradually dissolved. She didn't want to live safely like a little robot high school student in Cosgrove while girls her age were being taken prisoner in the county right next door. And as the fear dissolved and dispersed slowly through her bloodstream, she felt more alive than she had ever felt since she was a little kid.

"This danger, you get used to it, don't you, Dad?" The electric cycle was so quiet she knew he heard her.

"Yeah. You do. But don't get like me."

"What do you mean?"

"I mean I'm starting to like it. I don't know if I could go back to a normal life."

"It's an addiction?"

He didn't answer, and she let it go.

The last mile was through sparse, abandoned fields overgrown with scrawny trees and vines twisting around themselves like bundles of silver wire. They stopped a quarter mile from the gate, hid the cycle and crept closer. There was a tall cast iron fence and a brick guard post near a central gate. Behind the fence they saw a huge oval drive with brick houses lined up around the edge like a college fraternity row. They walked in the woods around the perimeter of the fence to see if there were any easier entrances at the sides, but there were no gaps in the fence, and no other entrances. The fence seemed impassible.

"Jesus Christ! Look. Barbed wire." Don was shocked. "It's gotta feel pretty hopeless, living in there."

"Maybe we could sneak past the guard some night."

"Hmm. Maybe *some* night. But we've got to get both Renee out of here and Sheila out of the packing plant on the *same* night, before they figure out that a resistance even exists."

Chapter 21

Joan seemed unhappy.

That was the only stick of evidence they had to go on. The new couple got to the service earlier each Sunday and moved closer to the front. They gave money, in cash, in an amount that didn't draw much attention. They noticed that Ezekial himself sweated profusely by the end of the service and almost tottered offstage under the close guidance of his bodyguard. His wife, Joan, waited for him, sometimes for half an hour, watching her children outside if it was good weather. Usually one sub-wife, recognizable by her Puritan habit, would be helping her wrangle the kids.

The two new congregants stuck to themselves. The man seemed much older than his wife, but this wasn't anything out of the ordinary among Ezekial's followers. Curiously, they both wore bangs covering half their foreheads. No one paid much attention when they wandered out the side door following Joan and her sub-wife and the gaggle of children.

It was a bright, warm, late October day. There was nothing for the children to do but run around on the large asphalt parking lot. There were seven children in all, but Joan simply told another woman, apparently the sub-wife, to take care of them. Most of the kids, though, seemed to be Joan's, and the younger ones tried to cling to her. She ordered the other wife to get them off and to entertain them.

Don and Amy edged nearer. Joan didn't notice them. She yelled at the other wife to chase after one of the boys who had run off the asphalt and was rounding the back of the church in the grass. The other wife disappeared after him. Joan was having a hard time keeping the other six children from fighting. It was five minutes before the other wife came back with the boy in tow.

"I told you to keep close watch on him!"

The other wife rolled her eyes. "I'm doing the best I ca …."

Joan slapped her.

There was no question about Joan's mental state.

Tears sprang to the other wife's eyes, but she held her head steady in a respectful pose. "I'm sorry, Ma'am. I am truly sorry. Please forgive me."

Another boy bolted for the grass. This time the new couple, Don and Amy, chased after him, and they each grabbed one hand and laughingly led him back to the group. Joan looked at them, her features frozen, as if she had been chastised by their example.

"Thank you. Thank you so much." Joan turned away and back toward the kids. "Lord forgive me," they heard her mumble. Then she turned back to Don and Amy, the distress in her eyes deepening the lines of her face. She talked directly to Don. "Look what's happening to me! Look what this is turning me into." She broke eye contact. "I shouldn't talk to you like that."

"Yes, you should." Don tried to sound interested and supportive. Like a real clergyman should be, he thought. "Why don't you sit down here on this bench and rest?"

Amy volunteered to go help with the children. Don sat down with Joan. "It's turning me into something awful," she blurted out. She spoke fast and low. "All this pressure on me – and all this power over the other wives. I'm taking everything out on them. This is *not me*."

"It's not the best situation. I can see that other wife is terrified of you."

"I wanted us all to be friends, since we have no choice but to live in this situation. But it's not a good situation for me to … *control* myself in. I mean, she's basically my slave – but she also sleeps with my husband."

"It's kind of barbaric, don't you think?"

She sighed. "… and I'm *his* slave. Sometimes I feel like I'm living in one of those terrorist camps. I get so angry, then I take it out on them."

Don took a chance. "Maybe there's a reason it feels like a terrorist camp. Your husband and the terrorists both justify what they do based on scripture written in barbaric times."

"Really?" Joan's eyes were pretty, green; her face up close was mapped by fine lines. "I've never really even read the bible. He's so sure of himself. I assume he knows what he's talking about."

"There's lots of contradictions in the bible. Most people interpret it in a more tolerant way than your husband does."

"Hmm." Her eyes were suddenly challenging. "I dare you to come to my house this afternoon and discuss this with my husband."

"My wife won't let me visit a polygamous household."

"You're scared of him, right? Everybody is scared of him. But I feel like I have nothing to lose." She turned away from him, looked out over the children playing on the parking lot, mumbled to herself. "Here I am, talking to a stranger like this."

"Not a stranger. A friend." She seemed startled, again, by his gentle tone. And he went on. "Maybe we can talk again after services next week. Right here. Alone. I mean outdoors, with my wife here, too."

✳✳✳ ✳✳✳

"Grant, do you want to have anything to do with your child, or not?"

Stacey had called him again. She knew he would have to report the call to Eleni, and that would put a strain on his relationship with his current lover. And there was not any urgent excuse for calling him again, as he had already promised he would help support the child when it came. In fact, he had already sent her a $1,000 check just to help with her current expenses.

"When the child comes, *if* it comes …." he started.

"What's this *if* business?"

"Sorry. I'm not pessimistic. I'm really not. It's just a habit. Living here in Massachusetts, if you're a man, you never know for sure if you're having a child until it's born."

It was a strange thing to say, and his tone was strange when he said it.

"I don't know why you said that. My pregnancy's going fine, if you don't count me feeling like shit half the time."

"So, do you need more money right now?"

"No. It's something worse than that. I'll just tell you. The Certainty Party has put in a new bill, MOMS-2. Women whose children were conceived outside of marriage will no longer be taken as concubines. Instead, their children will be taken away from them and given out to church members. Um … unless the biological father marries the mother before the birth."

"Oh, shit! Is there any chance of it getting a two-thirds majority?"

"Maybe. The Certainty Party is of course in favor of it. The Independents are all solidly against it – or at least they will be when I get through with them."

"You're their leader now?"

"Well, I have a lot of influence with them since I got the branding law repealed. It was just a special circumstance that time. I lucked out. But they don't know that."

"You can't do the same for MOMS-2?"

"Um, it's not working out that way at all. A lot of the Democrats and Republicans are signing on. They're close to two-thirds. All the pro-business people are hemming and hawing all over the place on this issue."

"So, it looks like it's going to pass?"

"Yep. What am I going to do, Grant? The Conception Control laws make it illegal for me to leave the state in my condition. So, I can't leave, and they'll take the baby away the minute it's born."

*** ***

Grant broke Massachusetts law that night by failing to reveal his conversation with Stacey to Eleni. It was not the kind of conversation you want to tell your lover. There were only a couple of options for him if MOMS-2 passed. He could do nothing, in which case the child he fathered with Stacey would be given away to an unknown churchman, never to be seen again by either Stacey or him. Or he could throw over Eleni, marry Stacey, and move to Kansas. But he was still appalled that Stacey had jumped into bed with Roland so quickly after their breakup. And there was no hotbed of internet companies, no start-up frenzy in Kansas, no company like Liotech where his legal expertise would be appreciated. He'd always said he'd rather die than live in Kansas. And his experiences in Kansas during the campaign hadn't made him feel any differently. Although the people there were nicer than he could ever have imagined, the laws there were unimaginably cruel.

Stacey of course was on a crusade against those laws. She was now the lynchpin of the Independent movement. She would never leave Kansas, even when she legally could. She was a hero to most of the women in Kansas. She was the person they were relying on to change the laws. He really couldn't ask her to leave them in the lurch.

Another option was a fake marriage. He could marry Stacey legally in Kansas, then go back to live his life in Boston. Of course, Eleni would leave him, and he'd essentially be single in Boston for the rest of his life. And Kansas might decide at some point it was not a real marriage and take their girl away anyway.

Chapter 22

She knew she couldn't get through to the billionaire busi-nessman right away, but she and Golsch shared enough se-crets that she was sure he'd eventually call back. He called her that evening. "How are you, Ms. Davenport?" His tone was cautious.

"Stacey. And can I call you Robert?"

"You may."

"Robert, I'll make this quick. There's a lot I need to clear up with you, and I think I need to do it in person."

"You want to blackmail me over my addiction, but you don't want to do it over the phone."

"Oh." She was stunned. "No. No. I would never do any-thing like that. Why would you think that?"

"Sometimes, especially in my personal life, it's hard to know what to think."

"Let me come and talk."

The limousine arrived outside of her apartment about 8:30 that evening. She sat alone. It was the same driver who had picked Golsch up from the cemetery after the funeral. Even through the slightly tinted glass she could recognize his wide shoulders, his shaved head. It was only a twenty-minute ride to his new condo in Golsch Towers. She let herself out of the limo and walked across the grandiose entranceway to the glass doors. She had brought all the identification Golsch's as-sistant had warned she'd need. Still, a staff member escorted her to the door of his penthouse suite on the twentieth floor. The condo itself had a sort of foyer, and there yet another assistant checked her credentials and escorted her to a large sitting room with a glass wall overlooking the spray of pin-point evening lights that was Topeka and, in the distance, the fading purple waves of the western sky.

"Mr. Golsch will be with you in just a moment." The assistant, a middle-aged woman in a tight black skirt, turned and walked away. Stacey sank into the soft cushions of the sofa and tried to brace herself.

Golsch walked quietly in and sat down in a leather chair opposite the sofa. There was a mahogany coffee table between them. Golsch looked like a different person than the man who had attended Roland's funeral. His hair, once as blonde as Roland's but now half grey, was neatly styled. The lines in his face weren't so deep, and he carried himself with an almost bouncy confidence that reminded her of his late son. He looked great, but Stacey's long history of addiction made her suspicious. This change had happened too quickly. She wondered what drug the "best doctors in the world," as he called them, had prescribed for him.

"Good evening, Ms. Davenport. I hope I haven't kept you waiting too long. I had a meeting in Washington this afternoon. I hope Bradbury, my driver, was on time to pick you up. Would you like something to drink?" His effusive speech was the clue. Was it amphetamines? Cocaine, even? Maybe some exotic synthetic she'd never even heard of.

"No, thank you. I'm fine."

He pulled back and seemed to gather control of himself. His eyes glittered.

"You know a big secret about me." His voice now seemed strangely calm. "I assure you that when you saw me, in the cemetery there, that was probably the lowest point of my life. My doctors and I have everything under control now."

"I hope you do. Look, I'm not here to blackmail you about being an addict. I would never do that."

"Okay. Good. Then why are you here?"

"I know firsthand what addiction is like. I'm here to thank you on behalf of all the addicts in Kansas. We don't have to be branded any more, thanks to your anti-branding bill."

He put his hands up. "I don't want my name associated in any way with that bill. Is that what you came here for, to put my name on it, or give me credit for it in the press?" He reached down and poured a drink for himself.

"Of course not. I just wanted to thank you. Thousands of addicts no longer have to live in fear of being burned, and having their faces mutilated."

He stood up and walked to the glass wall. Instinctively, she watched his legs for signs of a tremor. None. He spoke toward the glass. "What my lobbyists were saying was true. No business wants to send its employees to a state where they may be branded." He turned to face her, his figure silhouetted against the evening sky. He was every bit as tall and slim as his son had been. "And of course, that bill put me out of danger of being branded myself. I appreciate your putting your name on the bill and getting the Independents on board."

"I know the new law protects you. I'm glad. It protects everybody."

He walked back to the chair and sat down, seeming relieved, though he still jiggled an ankle. "You came all the way out here to thank me. That was very kind of you. You could have just called. Would you like something to drink now?"

"No." Stacey cleared her throat. "But there's something else. This is hard to say. When we talked in the cemetery, I think you got the wrong idea about something."

"Oh?" Golsch put his drink down; but then he didn't seem to know what to do with his hands.

"I'm sorry to have to tell you this. But I have to. My baby – she's not Roland's baby. So, she won't really be your granddaughter."

When he finally found his voice, it was flat, dead. "You didn't tell me at the grave. You saw my misapprehension as another way to take advantage of me?"

Stacey sat back. Her mouth dropped open. She had never

before met someone buried so deeply under so many layers of cynicism. They were hardly talking the same language. Her hand shook as she reached for the decanter and poured herself two fingers of whatever whiskey he was drinking. But before she could take a gulp, she slammed the glass down. She wanted the artificial courage the alcohol would bring, but she knew she had to dig deeper and find the courage within herself.

"Maybe you can't understand," she began. "But I held back in the cemetery because I was worried about you. It was already the worst day of your life. You were in every kind of pain, but you were holding onto that one string of hope – that you would have a grandchild. I couldn't take that one last thing away from you – not when you were in that condition."

"You were concerned about *me*?"

The wrinkled cynicism in his face seemed to soften just a notch as he considered this possibility. His accusatory glare was gone, but he couldn't look her in the eyes. He hadn't become a billionaire oligarch by being vulnerable, but he looked a little vulnerable right then.

Stacey saw that she had led him into an emotional no man's land, and she had to hold herself back from reaching across the table and touching his hand. Let the billionaires be billionaires, she thought; she had come only to speak the truth. But then she reached out and touched him anyway. Their eyes met for an instant before he looked away again. She stood up and excused herself, apologizing for being the bearer of bad news.

* * * * * *

Stacey tried to call Martha on her way back to her apartment, but Martha didn't pick up. She suspected Martha would have blackmailed Golsch, holding her knowledge of his addiction over his head until he promised to kill MOMS-2. She wasn't sure exactly why she hadn't done it herself. She stayed awake much of the night second guessing herself. By 5:00 a.m. she had given up on going back to sleep. She poured herself a cup of decaf coffee in her combination kitchen-dining room as the sky gradually lightened. She sat on a bare wooden chair and blankly stared out the glass wall at the silent apartment parking lot in the weak morning rays. It came to her just then that Golsch was probably the person who had paid her rent.

She had to defeat MOMS-2 or she would lose her daughter the moment she was born. But Golsch had not sponsored MOMS-2, and he wasn't even supporting it yet. He still seemed devastated that he had just lost his only son. And she had just told him he would never have a granddaughter. Three months ago, things had seemed so black and white that she hadn't hesitated to betray her friend Frieda to save the women of Kansas from servitude. MOMS-2 was just as bad, but the landscape seemed to have changed. The wave of passion she had first felt for Roland was no longer there to help her gloss over the personal harm she might be causing others. She would have to be a better person this time, in this fight.

When she arrived in their suite, Martha cornered her behind her desk. Martha was incredulous. "You didn't try to talk him out of supporting MOMS-2?"

"We didn't get that far. I thanked him for supporting the anti-branding bill." Stacey had never told Martha that Golsch had a personal reason for supporting the anti-branding bill. She wasn't sure why she was still keeping Golsch's addiction a secret from Martha. Part of it was probably addict-to-addict loyalty. Part of it was Golsch's inconsolable loss. But she was uneasy that she was treating Martha as a political ally when what she really needed was a friend.

"But MOMS-2! That's worse than branding. If it passes, you're going to lose your own child."

"The Certainty Party can pass that bill at any time. But, of course, they can't override a veto unless the rest of the legislature, most of whom are beholden to Golsch, votes along with them. That's why they're just holding the bill in committee. Golsch's people haven't committed."

"So, why didn't you talk to him about it?"

"You don't get it, Martha. Golsch is not my friend. He blames me for leading Roland astray." She caught Martha's eye and suddenly changed course. "And *you do, too*. You blame me for leading Roland astray." She didn't care if she sounded like she was whining. "Admit it, Martha."

Martha began in a modulated, practiced, political voice. "I did feel that Roland was doing a wonderful job holding together all the people who believed in women's rights." Then she swallowed hard. "And I guess I also feel he would have kept up the fight, and we wouldn't have lost him ...." Martha's face started to crumble. "We wouldn't have lost him, if you hadn't come along."

Stacey tried to pull her into a hug, but Martha resisted.

"I'll give you credit." Martha met her eyes but kept her distance. She seemed to shrug off her pain at Roland's death and snap back to her everyday practical self. "We Independents talk about these issues all the time, but you live them in your actual life."

"My life is a mess."

"But you're out there, living all the beauty and horror that is present day Kansas. I watched your campaign. You never gave up, no matter what happened. I admire that."

Chapter 23

The meeting that Joan proposed between Don and Reverend Ezekial never took place, but Don and Amy took the opportunity to meet Joan again in the parking lot outside of the church the next week. Joan was again supervising a subordinate wife as they tried to control seven restless children who had been cooped up in the church all morning. Amy immediately jumped in to help, and Joan obviously was trying harder to control her temper. She turned to Don, who had sat down right next to her.

"She's so young," she said, nodding towards Amy. "Is she your concubine?"

This was a weakness in their plan. Amy was just going to have to pass for her father's wife. They had decided just to power through any questions. "I have only one wife, Ma'am. I don't believe in that concubine stuff."

"Well," – Joan glanced around quickly, as if there were people close enough to overhear – "I'm not sure I believe in it either. He was such a sweet husband, when it was just the two of us. We had six children of our own. Then something happened. I guess God started to speak to him, and after that nothing I said mattered."

"I noticed last Sunday you didn't seem too happy with the situation."

"I have no rights," she breathed out harshly. "I hate my life. I'm starting to take it out on the other wives. You caught me last Sunday slapping one of them. You've got to believe me, I've never done that before. But I find myself wanting to hurt them, all the time. This isn't the kind of Christian I was raised to be."

"How many other wives are there?"

"Five."

"Do you hate them all?"

She caught his eye with a sharp look. "You don't understand. Some of them are really sweet. It's the *situation* I hate. We're all slaves – but I used to be free until they came."

"Any of them have red hair?"

"What? Yes. There is one. The latest girl. She has very red hair. Why do you ask?"

Don sighed, looked away. "I just have a niece who .... I doubt it's her."

"No, tell me."

*** ***

Robert Golsch had made sure she was ushered right in to his elaborate office. "Stacey, I'm glad to see you." But then his smile faded. "I hope this doesn't mean you changed your mind and decided to blackmail me after all."

"Do you think so little of me, really? Do you think I'm that kind of person?" When he didn't answer, she went on. "Can I sit down?"

Golsch started to stand up behind his massive desk, but then stopped halfway when he saw that Stacey had already sat down. He stayed in that awkward position for a second before he sat down himself. "I don't really know you. I didn't mean to sound so blunt. It sometimes helps in business." His look was suddenly tentative. "But the last time you were here, I don't know, it didn't feel like it was all business."

"I didn't mean it to be business. I mean, you had a right to know who was and who was not your granddaughter."

"Thank you for that. I needed to know that." Stacey could see tension in the lines of his face. He wasn't used to talking about his personal life. "Um, so, why are you here now, Stacey? Oh, sorry. I should offer you a drink – though maybe you shouldn't drink too much alcohol in your condition."

"You are blunt, aren't you? But you're right. Can I have a

glass of water?"

Golsch pressed a button on his desk and his office assistant came in almost immediately with two glasses of ice water. Stacey took a sip.

"I realize I don't have the *status* you thought I had the last time we met. I mean, the baby I'm carrying is not your granddaughter. I was sorry to have to tell you that."

"I understand. You had to do that. You have morals."

"Thank you. But this is like, a *political* visit. I'm here to ask you to oppose MOMS-2. As you know, I'm not married, and if that law passes, my baby will be taken away. I know the baby is not a blood relative of yours, but you've got to realize how much taking her away from me will hurt."

Golsch nodded, his face grim. "Yeah, I can see that would hurt."

"And it will hurt a lot of others, too. So, why do you support laws like this?" Stacey challenged him. "Don't you ever think of all the people this would hurt."

Golsch sat back. "This is a political process. My people – lobbyists, consultants – tell me what compromises I have to make to get legislation passed. I make those compromises. That's how laws are made."

"I'm just going to say this. Your so-called 'compromise' last September would have put me, and my sister, into servitude if MOMS had gone into law."

Golsch leaned forward, arms on his desk up to his elbows. The look in his eyes reminded Stacey of Roland's gaze when she had caught him up in some plan that was dead wrong. His words seemed memorized, his voice almost robotic. "People see my companies making hundreds of millions, and they think I'm just greedy and want more. But the whole business structure in this country is falling behind the rest of the world. We're competing against countries that have no regulations, no minimum wage."

Stacey was ready for that argument. "That's bullshit. I've researched it. Every one of your companies pays every one of your employees more than the minimum wage. Abolishing the minimum wage would have no effect on any of your businesses."

Stacey's attack seemed to shock Golsch out of his trance-like state. "It's more a philosophy, an ideology," he admitted. "I've become kind of a spokesman for that. Is that so bad?"

"Don't you have any women in your life who you love?"

Golsch suddenly stood up, walked out from behind his desk, stared out through the wall of windows. "That's a good question," he said to the city below.

*** ***

"I'm about to commit a criminal act in the state of Massachusetts," Grant began his phone call.

"Don't do it on my behalf." Stacey was peeved, frustrated, flippant.

"I'm going to tell you about Eleni's doctor's appointment."

"Don't do that," she snapped. "Wait. She doesn't have cancer or something?"

"She had an abortion."

"I don't want to hear this." There were so many reasons why Stacey didn't want to hear this.

"I can't talk to anybody here. She had the perfect legal right to do it, I know. She didn't even have to tell me, but she did. She's a very honest person."

"None of this is any of my business."

"Please listen to me. I mean, I'm glad that she's ... *fertile* and all that. It means we could probably have kids if we ever got married. But, Stacey, she didn't tell me she was pregnant – like you did."

"This is a problem between you and her, Grant. It's not

my problem."
"I know. I know. Thank you for letting me talk about it."
"Goodbye, Grant."

Chapter 24

Ruth was meeting Sheila a few minutes before work in the boning room. Sheila's eyes were begging. "When you get your sister out, can you take me, too?"

"Shhh. I'll try to get as many women out as I can. You'll be easy. Just hop in the truck when it's time."

"I can tell you don't have children."

Ruth looked up. She didn't have children. But she didn't know exactly what that comment meant. "I don't. What do you mean?"

"I can't leave my little boy in their hands. If I escape by myself, I'll never see him again."

"Oh. Don't you live in Bible Land where Renee is being kept?"

"No. It's an hour away from there. Way out in the country."

"Got the address?"

"No. I'm not allowed to know exactly where it is. It's probably just an RFD number anyway. And there's no windows in the van, so I can't follow the turns."

"Shit!"

Realizing how loud she had shouted, Ruth grimaced. They both looked around to see if anybody had heard. Ruth went on in a whisper. "Maybe I can get you a GPS tracker. You can put it on underneath the van. Bring it back to me once you've made a round trip."

"You are so wonderful! Are there a lot of people like you out there – I mean resisters?"

"A few. And there's probably a lot of sympathetic people like the Greek. You know, I might ask *him* to get me the manifest from the van to see if they have the addresses where they pick you women up every day. That might even be an easier way than using a GPS. If he'll do it."

Sheila slipped out the side door, but not soon enough to avoid being seen by Ziba, who was watching from the bench under the overhanging shed roof where they always ate lunch. It would be too dangerous for Sheila to talk to Ruth again that day. Sheila couldn't figure out how to warn her that Ziba was still watching.

Ruth pulled the Greek into the chiller and sealed the door. She was blunt. "These contract women are all slaves. Just like your daughter told you. Would you help me save them?" She was taller than him; she stepped back so she could see his expression. His calm manner, the sympathetic look in his large, dark eyes – now fastened on hers – told her she hadn't made a mistake. Three hours later, at her morning break, he slid her a copy of the complete manifest from the contract workers' delivery van. The address of each woman was listed next to her new biblical name.

She smiled at this good man. "I think I can get Sheila and her son out. You might need to hire a new offal scraper." The Greek touched her on the shoulder, his smile changing to a look of concern.

But Ruth knew she couldn't save Renee from the fortified prison of Bible Land with just a pickup truck and a pistol. The pickup truck was really just for rescuing Sheila and her son, Bobby. Now knew where to find Bobby. That plan could probably be started right now, but Don kept telling her to wait. He had come up with a plan for saving Renee, but it was much more complicated, and he kept telling Ruth not to make any moves until she heard from him.

* * * * * *

Damien was afraid of them now. Their relationship had changed the instant he confessed. His information about the Genesis Riders did not come from overhearing them gossiping and bragging in the store. His information came from his roommate, or "barnmate," Dirk, who was a Genesis Rider himself.

"Are you some kind of fucking double agent?" Don accused him, getting into his face, giving Damien a close look at the scar on his forehead. Ruth unholstered her Glock and raised it toward Damien.

"No, no. It's not like that! We share the barn, right? My Dad's charging me rent. Dirk was in the store here one day and said he had no place to live. He offered to split the rent." Damien was shaking, and talking fast. "He's not a friend of mine. I mean, he's okay, but I would never do any of that brutal crap that they do. You gotta believe me! I haven't told him anything. He has no idea you guys even exist."

The silence of Don and Ruth and Amy shut him up. The fluorescent lights buzzed overhead. Amy was the first to act. She put her hand out and tried push the barrel of the gun down, but Ruth jerked it away. Amy then turned to her father, but his eyes were locked on Damien's. Finally, she broke the silence. "Listen, Dad, Ruth. If Damien was working for the Riders, he could have already sold Ruth and I to them weeks ago. He could have made money by betraying us. Instead, he's been helping us."

"We don't need anybody who's been lying to us," Don insisted.

"He was scared to tell us before. Who's never told a lie, Dad? Right, Dad? Look, guys, we have to trust somebody, sometime." As Amy's logic seemed to sink in, and the others kept silent, the color slowly returned to Damien's face.

Ruth stepped closer to Damien "All this stuff you've been telling us about the Riders? It's just what you overheard from this guy, Dirk. Right?"

"I ... um ... yes."

"Everybody else in this room is risking their lives to save

these women."

"Uh-huh. Okay." Damien seemed to be trying to say as little as possible.

"You're the only one here who has access to the Riders, and their plans."

"Uh-huh."

"What she's saying," Amy pushed Ruth's gun gently aside. Looking up directly into Damien's eyes, she pleaded. "You've already helped us a lot, and we really appreciate it. But we really need more information. Do you think you can step it up a little? Please."

Damien's voice dropped a note deeper. "I guess I could try."

*** ***

A week later, when they quizzed him, he didn't know the names of any more Genesis Riders, nor did he have a single new motorcycle license number. But he obviously had found out something about the Riders, and he was obviously shaken by it.

"I know where their clubhouse is. Dirk brought me there," he explained. "I told Dirk I'd do some work for them."

"What work?" Don demanded. The three of them stared at Damien.

"I told Dirk I'd set up a wireless door lock and alarm system for them."

"Why the hell would you do that?"

"To find out where it is. Listen, it's in a converted barn, on an old, run-down farm one of the guys inherited. He looks like a meth head. The hayloft is converted to rooms – just like my place, except their barn is grey. Anyway, they were bragging. They told me they bring the women there when they first take them from their homes."

"Is my sister there?" Ruth's eyes on him were suddenly

bright green mirrors.

"Nobody's being held in the clubhouse right now."

"So, where is this barn?" Don didn't seem impressed with the story so far.

"I'll tell you. But wait." He stared towards the women. "I brought a lot of wires, batteries and other shit with me, including a surveillance camera. I was going to put it in backwards in the clubhouse so we could spy on them, but they were all over me in there, so I couldn't. I just put in the lock with the key code, like I originally promised Dirk.

"But when it was time to pay me, they didn't give me any money. They sent me to this little white shed off to the side. They called it Penance. There was a girl in there. They said I had thirty minutes to do anything I wanted to her. She was tied down to hooks screwed into the floor. They said she'd do anything for a sip of water from a cup that was just beyond her reach. That was just one of the tortures they had been doing to her."

"Don't tell us any more," Amy groaned.

"Wait. I gave her the water. I had to pour it in her mouth. But I had brought all my gear in with me because I didn't trust those guys. When I saw what they were doing .... Anyway, now I got 24-hour streaming of what's going on in Penance. It's all being recorded in the cloud. I brought a six-hour sample." He paused. "But you might not want to look at it."

"What else did you do to her?" Ruth broke the silence this time.

"Nothing. Look, when I got back to the clubhouse, I had to talk like I raped her. They thought it was funny. But there's only a few who do the Penance on the women. Mostly Hunter, the big one they're all afraid of. Dirk, my barnmate, doesn't do that."

"That woman could be my sister!" Ruth cried.

Damien met her eyes. "Your sister has red hair, right? No,

it's not her. The girl I saw is gone now anyway, and there's been no one else as of this afternoon."

"Didn't you ask her name?"

"I did. She gave me some biblical shit name nobody uses any more. She was too scared to give me her real name. But she definitely wasn't your Renee."

* * * * * *

Renee was learning the rules of Ezekial's house in Bible Land. As the sixth wife, she was required to obey all the previous wives – except Dina, who was a servant to all. She also had to obey the orders of all the children over the age of seven. All of the older children were Joan's. Renee was responsible for the care and discipline of any of the younger children when they were in her presence. If a child cried for her mother, she was to tell her that she was her mother also. The children were taught to love, fear and obey their father Ezekial as God's one and only true prophet.

There were four young children and two toddlers, though the six wives were working hard at producing more. All the captives were pregnant. Renee didn't dare ask anyone if Ezekial was the father. She cherished the fact that she was already pregnant by her boyfriend and it would be at least six months before she would have to be carrying Ezekial's child. Even with all the work required to teach the children, tend the toddlers, prepare the meals and clean the house, there wasn't always enough work to keep all six wives busy. Renee had heard that some men hired their wives out to do contract work, but Mara told her not to hope for that.

"He says he wants us to focus on God's work," Mara explained. "That means his household, and his businesses. And his penis. He wants to keep the six of us even more hidden than the other kidnapped women."

They were in their bedroom, the only shared bedroom in

the house. They both liked the arrangement. At night, they got to lie together on Mara's mattress and talk.

"He hasn't called for me yet. I mean at night," Renee confided.

"I'm keeping him pretty busy."

"He's so old. How can you stand it?"

"Ha. It's kind of funny, all the stuff he doesn't know."

"You enjoy this?"

"I like seeing him beg." Mara closed her eyes, resting her head on the pillow. Her next whisper was hardly audible. "I wish I was dead."

Chapter 25

We're having a little ceremony to honor my son, just a few people. I'd be honored if you would come.

Stacey stared at the handwritten invitation for a full minute before she got up and took it to Martha's office.

"Golsch has invited me to something, a memorial I guess, for Roland."

Martha caught the concerned look in Stacey's eyes. "Is he going to publicly admit Roland was his son?"

"I don't know how public. He said just a few people. But, who am I? Does he think I'm part of his family now? Do you think Frieda will be there?"

Stacey hadn't felt so bewildered by a social situation since she was in middle school. In high school, she hadn't been involved in any situation that didn't involve drugs, and in college she had slowly picked her friends, one by one. Now she felt like she was back in middle school, asking a friend what to do. But at least she had a friend, and Martha seemed to live a normal life and might know how to deal with these things.

"I don't know, Stacey. It could be an ambush."

Stacey clasped her hands together. "So, what's the worst-case scenario?" She knew she sounded assured, but she didn't really know if her politician's instincts applied to social occasions like this.

"Here's the worst-case scenario. Frieda is there, and she screams at you that you led him into sin and got him killed. And his mother is there and screams the same thing."

"The same thing you wanted to scream at me."

Martha dropped her hands to her desk. "That was before I knew you. Before you told me the whole story. I know you now. You did what you had to do."

"Thanks." Stacey collapsed into a chair across from her

new friend. "You know, my instinct is to just go. See how Golsch is doing. I don't get the feeling he hates me."

"Maybe you should trust your instinct."

*** ***

The service was not religious. It was held in the presidential suite of the Kansas Hedge Suites, the new hotel that Golsch Industries had built in Topeka. The room was lined tastefully with small vases of red roses, a table was set up with pictures of Roland at every stage of his life, excerpts from some of his speeches were framed around the walls. Robert Golsch was there, as well as Roland's mother, a few of her friends, a few people Stacey had never met, and Frieda, who was sitting alone.

Stacey sat down next to Frieda. "I'm truly sorry for your loss." The last time Stacey had spoken to Frieda was at her own wedding to Roland, where she had recited the second wife's vows before both Frieda and Roland. It had been a humiliating ceremony for both of them, as Frieda was forced to help her husband take a second wife, and Stacey was forced to place herself in servitude to both Frieda and Roland. Stacey had run out at the last minute, and Roland had been killed pursuing her. Reverend Ezekial himself had been performing the wedding in accordance with his own doctrines of the subordination of women. Frieda had been a devoted follower of Ezekial, and her appearance at the wedding was proof that she then accepted his teachings as the word of God. Stacey had no idea what Frieda thought now.

At least her hairstyle was of the current millennium, a severe blonde bob that emphasized her intelligent grey eyes, her angular body, her straight, tall posture. Stacey wore her chestnut hair long. Her body had softer curves, complete with the first swellings of her baby bump. She had to sit tall to look her former friend in the eye. "I mean I'm sorry for *everything* you lost, including what I took from you."

"He's home with God now."

Although Frieda's religious belief was sincere, Stacey was surprised there wasn't a trace of sadness in Frieda's pronouncement – and not a hint of anger at her. But what had Frieda lost, really, other than an uninterested, controlling husband who was deeply in love with someone else – and who had promised to confine her, wife number one, to "clean quarters" so he could spend all his time with Stacey? Roland had always said that Frieda had no interest in him, other than as her husband, ordained to be her master by the laws of God as interpreted by Ezekial. She had now lost her position in the familial role that Ezekial had ordained for all women – but, now that she was a widow, there was nothing to stop her from regaining that role again with some other man. Maybe Frieda was not as broken up about Roland's demise as his parents were.

Stacey chastised herself for having such shallow thoughts. She remembered seeing Frieda weeping at the graveside. That was more than Stacey had done. Stacey thought Roland had turned into a monster. She had witnessed his death close up, but once the shock and revulsion had worn off, she was not sorry that he was gone. Frieda had not seen that side of Roland. She obviously had at least some feelings for him. Stacey tried to explain why she had gotten engaged. "I only agreed to marry him because he said he would sign off on MOMS if I didn't."

Stacey had no idea back then whether Frieda cared about MOMS. She still had no idea. But Stacey did want Frieda to know why she had agreed to become Roland's second wife. It had been the only way to defeat that bill. She waited for a response now, but Frieda just nodded slightly, acknowledging that she had heard. Stacey could not figure out what was going on in that woman's mind.

Stacey stood up and started to approach Roland's mother. Medium height, round, sagging face, short curled hair, giant tortoise shell glasses, Mrs. Asher looked like what she was, a single mother who had been managing the lower office operations of a massive business for years without much help from upper management. Stacey knew that Golsch had supported her well financially, but he had never married her. And he had never acknowledged he was Roland's father.

Until now. Golsch approached Mrs. Asher and slowly guided her to the tiny podium. Golsch spoke briefly about the loss of his son, depicting some of the precious moments they had shared as father and son. There was no mention, of course, of the seamier side of the relationship, the one that only Stacey and Mrs. Asher were aware of. But that had long ago been forgiven. Mrs. Asher acted not the least bit in awe of her billionaire boss. They were just equal parents of a son who had died. Mrs. Asher was the only one who cried, but Golsch bowed his head in obvious pain.

Stacey had not been asked to speak. She never got to talk to Mrs. Asher alone. There was also one man from the Independent political group there. Stacey didn't know him well. He gave a low-key speech praising Roland's leadership of the party. Stacey tried to talk to him later, but he was cold to her. He was the only person there who still seemed to blame her for Roland's tragic end. Robert Golsch didn't approach her until near the end of the affair.

"Thank you for coming," he said. "You knew him better than most people here. Your being here makes it complete, somehow. Realistic. Truthful." He lowered his voice. "You know all the dirt, and still you came."

"I believed at first he was going to be a great man. But that jealousy ...."

"Apparently, you took the brunt of that jealousy. He dragged you through the dirt. And, since then, you've been kinder to me than you needed to be. I want to thank you for that."

"Look, I promised I wouldn't talk politics here, but how could you let MOMS-2 get so far in the legislature? Do you realize what it does? They will take away my baby if that gets enacted into law."

"Oh." He pulled back a fraction of an inch, and she could see his political self kick in. "I'm not committed either way on MOMS-2. I probably won't support it, but I need the leverage that the uncertainty provides me."

Stacey stamped her foot. "No, you don't! You don't need anything. Your one of the richest men in the world. But I need to know, and thousands of other women need to know, that we can keep our own children!"

"I've never seen that fire in you before. No wonder you've gotten so far in politics."

She got up close, whispered harshly. "Don't patronize me. With this MOMS-2 thing, you're doing worse to me than Roland ever did. And you don't even have the excuse of being insanely in love with me." She stepped back. "I thought you understood now about parents, and children. I thought we were friends."

People were staring, and he left her side then. She got her breath and gathered up her things and left. Golsch was not the person she'd expected to have a confrontation with. And that was because, she suddenly realized as she walked across the hall to the elevator, she actually had thought they were friends.

As the elevator door started to close, Golsch suddenly stepped in and let the door close behind him. "Okay," he said, in his billionaire's calm voice that could quiet an entire room. "I want us to be friends." He brushed his fingers through his greying hair. "We are friends. MOMS-2 is dead as of this minute."

Chapter 26

They were still making love in the conference room at work and in their own places at night. He felt like he was in college again, where he played at romance with girl after girl. But Eleni was no girl. She was a smart, self-assured and independent woman. She was ambitious and idealistic. And she loved to play as much as he did.

"I have good news," she surprised him one night as they were lying together on the bed right after one of their sessions. "I got the feeling you didn't like it when I had that abortion."

"Um … yes. But I knew it was none of my business."

"Well, that won't happen again."

"What do you mean?"

"I got an implant. Look, feel my arm. It's under the skin. I can't believe you didn't notice it tonight." She guided his hand to the cylindrical lump he could barely feel under the skin near her triceps.

"Wow. Thank you. That did bother me a little, that you were … *doing it* that way. But I knew it was none of my business."

"I guess I believe that everything I do is some of your business. But I didn't tell you the best part. Guess how long the implant is good for."

"Six months, I heard."

"That's the old implants. The new ones can be for as long as you want."

"No kidding. So, how long did you choose?" He leaned up on his elbow.

She sat up quickly. He was distracted for a second by her breasts.

"Thirteen years."

"Oh." He lost interest in her breasts.

"So, I'm safe from getting pregnant until I'm 37."

He lay back with her and stroked her body almost absent-mindedly while staring at the ceiling. "So, we can have all the fun, fun, fun we want."

It became harder to arrange their lunchtime trysts. One day they decided not to lock the door and instead invited their co-workers to lunch together with them in the conference room. People had such a good time they began to ask if they could do it again. Eleni caught Grant's attention and rolled her eyes at this. She had predicted this would happen. They steered the conversation into having lunch there "maybe once a week or so." People agreed on that; but ever since that first day, there was constant conversation in the office about what day would be lunch day in the conference room. Grant and Eleni tried to get people to pin themselves down to a date two or three weeks in advance, but it seemed there was always somebody who couldn't make it and wanted the day to be changed at the last minute. But the constant tension only made their remaining trysts in the conference room seem more exciting.

"One day we'll get caught," she laughed. This was a few days after the implant, and it seemed like a burden had been lifted from her mind.

"We're good. We have Amos's permission. We're signed on with the company as sexual partners." He pulled at her clothes and helped as she wriggled out of them.

"You're crazy if you think Amos is going to protect us. What he's doing could be considered as giving favorable treatment to a legal assistant who is sexually servicing his in-house counsel. Every other woman who ever applied for a legal assistant job here can sue him for sexual discrimination. If another applicant sues, he's going to blame us. He won't protect us, in the end."

She stayed on this subject all the while he took his clothes off, but her ferocity was not dampening his spirits at all. "Can we not talk about that right now?" He stopped her monologue with a kiss.

She pulled back with a smile. "I'm telling you, that little lock on the door is going to cause trouble someday."

*** ***

She is really good. There's absolutely nothing I can criticize about her.

Grant found himself repeating this phrase about Eleni more and more over the next few weeks. He kept telling himself if he could design the perfect woman for himself, she would be it. He found himself daydreaming of changing his career so he could live out his life wherever this beautiful woman wanted to go.

Unfortunately, there were a lot of previous moments in his life that impinged on his dreams. He had been forever changed by watching Stacey go up against the Certainty Party and the Genesis Riders in Kansas. He knew the abductions and rapes were still taking place in Neola County. He knew Ruth's sister was still a captive concubine. He knew Ruth still carried a gun, and he still wondered if she'd someday blow her stack and go after Reverend Ezekial himself. Mostly, though, he started to wonder if he was enough of a man to be a good father to his baby. He'd been ambivalent about Stacey's pregnancy from the start, first running away, then considering being involved, then insisting that he be involved to the point where he almost caused a civil war in Kansas.

Then, he had been angry enough about Stacey's seedy compromises to leave her to her own devices. But he still kept watch on the political situation in Kansas. When MOMS-2 was proposed, which meant that his own child would be assigned to a random fundamentalist clergyman in Kansas, he waited for Stacey to call – but when she had, his bitterness over the whole history of her affair with Roland had washed over him, and he had brushed her off. Now MOMS-2 was no longer a threat, but he still couldn't get Stacey and their child out of his mind. He had never realized he wanted children until Eleni decided it couldn't happen for another 13 years. His child with Stacey would be 14 years old by then.

He called Stacey one night while Eleni was at her law school classes. "Congratulations on squelching MOMS-2. I hear you persuaded Golsch to drop the whole thing."

"Thank you. Now, I guess if you come to Kansas you can at least take a quick look at your child."

He was put off by her sarcasm. "Our child."

"But you're not coming to Kansas, are you?"

"I can't live there."

"MOMS never passed. We repealed the branding law. MOMS-2 is gone. I think things are getting better in Kansas."

"Stacey, you ignored my messages, you started an affair right away, you got publicly engaged to a married man. I tried to understand all that. And I still worked hard for your election."

"I never got to thank you for that."

"You're the only person I would do that for."

"Thank you. You believed in me." He could hear her sigh. "Honestly, Grant, part of what kept me going, all along, was trying to be as strong as you thought I was."

"As I *think* you are. Present tense."

"But you're not coming to Kansas."

"I don't know, Stacey. My whole life is here."

"Including Eleni. I guess under blue state laws you have to report this phone call to her."

Chapter 27

Mothers were allowed a half hour a day with their own children. Once a week, they could have this visit in their own rooms. But it was still three weeks before Renee met Seth, Mara's two-year-old son.

"Hello, Seth. I'm … Tamar." Even a two-year-old could blab. Better to use her new Ezekial-given name with the child. Seth wasn't shy. That seemed to be a characteristic of the kids in the household, raised as they were in a group by almost-interchangeable mother figures, in a mini-society where everyone had to think the same thing. Seth smashed his toy Jesus into Renee's face just as readily as he had smashed it into Mara's.

"Who is his father?"

Mara looked at her. "I used to be a barmaid. There used to be a lot of drugs, a lot of drunk parties. The guy – he's a guy I wouldn't even talk to if I was sober."

"Oh my God!"

"I'm trying to forget his name. After I got pregnant, the best offer I had was passage to a blue state. But I wouldn't take it. Who's your baby daddy?"

"My boyfriend, Jeff. We were supposed to be married in January."

"Oh." Mara put her arm around Renee's shoulders. "Hang in there, kid. Maybe he'll find you."

"I hope so." But she didn't really have much hope. Renee rested her head on Mara's shoulder. The other woman's long, coarse, dark hair tickled her face. She found herself pressing her face against Mara's neck. She had missed being touched. "I don't think my Jeff will ever find me. What are we going to do?"

"We're going to take care of each other." Mara patted her

on the head but pushed her gently away as she focused her attention on Seth.

"What's his real name?" Renee asked after he had been taken back to the nursery.

"Jimbo."

Renee laughed. "That's just as crazy as Seth."

"Maybe so, but it's *my* crazy."

They had to teach the children hymns that afternoon.

We are God's holy children servants.
We pray to serve Him well.
We listen to God's holy prophet.
We will not go to hell.

Mara rolled her eyes. "God, what I wouldn't give for iTunes."

"What I wouldn't give for a drink."

"Shhh!"

Dina came through the doorway just then, head bowed, being careful to walk by without disturbing the children. She held her head so still her dirty blonde ponytail was not even swinging. "What?" Renee whispered. "Is she a spy, too?"

"We don't know. She's trained to do exactly what Reverend E wants, and nothing else. And she would spy if they asked her to." Mara half turned away but kept whispering. "Word is he doesn't use her at all. Apparently, fucking a robot doesn't turn him on."

That night, Ezekial called for Renee for the first time. She walked obediently, head bowed, to his room. She knew if she showed the slightest bit of resistance she would be sent to Penance. But she couldn't pretend to be happy, or intrigued, as Mara had recommended. Ezekial was not attractive to her with his middle-aged paunch and the roadmap of lines on his face. She tried to smile as she readied herself for him. She gasped when he started.

"No," he commanded. "Pray!" he commanded. "Praise your Jesus for this blessing!"

"Oh Jesus, oh Jesus, oh Jesus," she repeated mechanically. With her boyfriend, three or four times was enough, but Reverend Ezekial seemed to take forever. Finally, he let out his own "Oh Jesus" and stopped. He didn't seem as thrilled with her as he should have been. Maybe she was just comparing him to her boyfriend, who actually looked at her when they were doing it.

"You are blessed." He said as he stood next to her, wiping himself with the bedspread. "The Bible says no one of illegitimate birth shall enter the assembly of the Lord. But your child will be cleansed of the stain of his unholy conception by the intercession of God's Holy Prophet Ezekial. Your child will learn the ways of God, and no other."

"Thank you so much, Reverend Ezekial. Praise be to you, Reverend Ezekial."

*** ***

"I have to see the governor, today." Stacey spoke from the doorway of the governor's outer office, not even bothering to sit down on the plush chairs set up before the desk of the governor's legislative assistant. "This is really an emergency."

"And you are …?" Toby Ratchenfeld, Governor Adams' chief legislative liaison, was pretending not to recognize the most famous face in the Kansas legislature.

"You know who I am. I have something with me that the governor needs to see immediately."

"The governor is at a conference in Kansas City today, and she is booked up with meetings all day tomorrow. If you'll just give the item to me, I'll be sure she sees it as soon as reasonably possible."

"No, you won't, Toby. I know Governor Adams has left standing orders that she doesn't want to be seen talking to any of the Independents until the next election cycle. I'm telling you that this is a video of a woman being tortured. In Kansas. As a part of a regular protocol. The governor needs to stop this."

Ratchenfeld made a face. "She's not here. And she's not available tomorrow. Now, if this piece of evidence is so important, I don't understand why you don't just leave it with me, and I will make sure it gets to the governor's attention as soon as possible."

"Because it's urgent."

Ratchenfeld sighed. "You see this stack of emails?" He gestured to a stack of papers more than an inch thick next to his computer. "Every one of these emails is urgent, according to the sender."

"Okay. Here's what I'm going to do. I'm going to leave this copy with you, and other copies are going to be sent to the Journal and the Star. If the press reports this, and then finds out the governor's office had it and did nothing about it, it will be on your head."

But she couldn't get anyone in the press interested in the video either. She then visited in person the deputy chief of the Kansas Bureau of Investigation, who was very interested until he learned the event took place in Neola County. "We're not allowed to go into Neola County. Governor's orders." He raised his eyes to hers. They were veined in red, they seemed tired. "What I can do, I can call the sheriff of Neola County and ask him to take a look."

"You know that's useless."

The deputy chief hung his head. "Why don't you try the governor?"

"I already have."

In desperation, she asked for a meeting with Robert Golsch. He granted her one the next day.

"This is a video," she began, "of a woman being bound

and tortured in a building in Neola County. You will see that the torture equipment was already in place, because this is a *regular occurrence* in that place. The Genesis Riders are doing this under the orders of Reverend Ezekial and his buddies in the church."

Golsch held up his hand. "I believe you. I don't want to see it. Let me call my lawyer to come over here right now."

The lawyer didn't want to see it either, but he was very interested. "Do you know this woman's name?"

"No."

"Does this happen as a regular occurrence?"

"Yes. You can see the room is set up for this kind of activity."

"Do you have any videotapes of anyone else?"

"No, the surveillance camera didn't catch anybody else, at least in the next forty-eight hours."

"Was this surveillance camera placed with the permission of the property owner?"

"I doubt it."

"Do you have the names of the ones doing the punishment?"

"No. All I have is this video, the exact address where it's happening, and the word around Neola County that this is the standard method of dealing with recalcitrant concubines."

"The KBI should go in and investigate." The lawyer stated the obvious.

"They won't. Governor's orders."

"Then what do you expect my client to do?"

She turned toward Golsch but spoke to his lawyer. "I don't know. He seems to be able to do anything in this state that involves pushing people around."

The lawyer braced, but Golsch smiled. Then his look changed to one of concern.

"Is this camera still connected?"

"Yes. It's a surveillance camera. It's continuously recording. The only thing different is that it's rigged to record everything to the cloud, and to a hard drive off the premises. We have real time as well as historical footage."

"But you haven't seen anyone else being abused?"

"Right."

"Stacey, this is awfully vague. Are there any reports of missing women in Neola County?"

"There are hundreds of missing women in Neola County. The Genesis Riders are taking them, but of course they're not so stupid they'd keep records of the names of their victims."

"I don't see what we can do." The lawyer interrupted. "We can't bring a civil suit without the name of the woman or the names of any of the abusers. I know a similar suit was brought in federal court enjoining the sheriff of Neola County to enforce the law, but the sheriff is apparently ignoring it. I don't think this information would add much to that – legally, I mean. The sheriff is the one who should be enforcing the law."

Golsch held his hands out to Stacey. "As powerful as I am in the economic and political circles, I have no powers of law enforcement at all, Stacey. If they do that to another woman, or if you get this woman's name, come back and I promise we'll try something."

"So, you're saying another woman needs to be tortured before you do anything?"

Golsch stared forward, his eyes distant, his mouth set in a hard line. "I'm saying we need more evidence."

*** ***

Stacey joined the group for a meeting after hours in Damien's record store. Damien had fast-forwarded the video from the last 24 hours. No other woman had been brought there for Penance in that time.

"If we can get someone to watch full-time, we can catch them in the act next time," Ruth suggested.

"And then do what?" Don scoffed. "Go in there with guns blazing? They'd wipe us out."

"Damien, is there any way you can get the names of the Genesis Riders we saw on that video?"

"No. I checked the records here. They always paid cash in this store ... and of course you know how they paid me for my security lock work."

"Doesn't Dirk know their names?"

"I tried. He got suspicious. He won't tell me."

"Okay. Okay." Don paced back and forth across the floor in front of the record counter, four steps each way. The others instinctively made room for him. "We're not going to take them down legally, and we don't have enough firepower to fight them. Let's go back to the original plan – save Ruth's sister, Renee. I think we can at least do that."

"You'd need several people with guns to do that," Ruth started. "And even if we got her out of Bible Land, the Genesis Riders would be all over us before we got to the county line."

"Yeah, it would be impossible for us to storm that building, but I have a plan. No, really, I do. Have I ever failed you guys yet?"

* * * * * *

Ruth had quietly learned the real names of two more of the contract workers at United Processing. She had promised Sheila she would save her and her son, but she couldn't promise the other two women anything except she'd give their information to their families. She asked the two women to keep an eye on Ziba, who kept whining that she was going to complain to her husband about the unholy goings on at the packing plant.

At home one night, using the manifest the Greek had given her, Ruth found Sheila's owner's location on Google maps. She committed the directions to memory. Ruth had all she needed. She arrived early at the plant every morning, nervous and ready to go, and contacted Don on the burner phone she had hidden under the seat of her truck. It seemed to be taking forever for him to give her the go-ahead.

Chapter 28

Eleni was on edge. They didn't usually meet in restaurants. Grant could trace the tension in her posture even as he felt the queasiness in his own stomach. He ordered a beer and she sipped at a glass of red wine. The waiter started to ask for their order but changed his mind when he sensed the strain in the air.

"Okay. I need to tell you something, Eleni. I had another phone conversation with Stacey."

"She called you again?"

"No. I called her."

She pressed both hands on the white linen tablecloth. Her shoulders stiffened as if she were hemmed in by these surroundings. They both realized at the same time that he had arranged the surroundings as an elegant trap. She had to listen. She couldn't make a scene. "What is it you want to tell me about her?" she said.

"I'm going to try to get back with her."

Eleni's mouth dropped open. She had worn a white dress sprinkled with a delicate flurry of sequins for this special occasion, and now the sparkles tracked her breathing as her chest rose and fell. Her eyes filled with tears. She didn't cry out, or whine, or drop eye contact. But he could read the loss written in her face.

"I still think you're a wonderful woman, and you're going to do great things," he whispered.

"Thanks. I guess." There was a hint of a sob in her voice now. "But you're leaving me." She put her glass to her lips, changed her mind, put it down. "Can I ask one question?"

He nodded.

"Was it the implant? The thirteen-year implant? I mean, I have definite plans, but maybe we could have compromised on that."

He noticed she used the past tense. She was really hurt, but she had too much pride to beg, or to try to talk him out of it.

"I could lie and say I'm already having a baby with Stacey and I can't get over that. But that's not all of it, really."

"What else?"

"I guess it's ...." The actual reason came to him in that instant. "She's not really a lawyer, you know. She doesn't play it safe."

"You mean she's out in the world. She's fighting. She's engaged."

"Ha, *engaged*. Well, maybe yes, she puts herself on the line." He thought he had to try to explain. "Look, I'm not saying I'm like that myself. I don't have that kind of courage. But I'm really attracted to hers."

Eleni seemed to relax a little and even took a sip of her wine. Then she put it down, spilling some of the red on the tablecloth. "This is so *sudden*." At that word, she blinked through more tears and went on. "But I know why you told me right away. You didn't want to be sneaking around behind my back." She dabbed her eyes with the restaurant's linen napkin. "As much as it hurts me, I don't blame her for trying to get you back. You are a good man, Grant. No girl in her right mind wouldn't try."

*** ***

The meeting at Damien's record store was the first time Stacey had seen her father since election night. She understood why he wanted to stay underground. People suspected that Don was the Evolutionary Guard, which had killed two Genesis Riders during the campaign and was suspected of killing Roland also. But there was no actual evidence connecting Don with that group, or with Roland's death. There were no eyewitnesses other than Stacey, who was not about to tell the Neola County authorities anything. The sheriff's office in Neola County was too compromised, too much publicly in league with the outlaw Genesis Riders, to be trusted to be fair.

After Roland was killed, the Genesis Riders had ridden in force to Cosgrove City, burned down her mother's house, shot the dog, and chased her family to the church shelter in town, where there was an armed standoff between the women seeking shelter and the Riders who were trying to kidnap them. Ruth and Stacey and Amy eventually faced them down, and the danger of civil war had receded. After that night, the Riders stuck to Neola County, and the Evolutionary Guard seemed to disappear. No one but Stacey knew that her father was the Evolutionary Guard.

"Dad, why didn't you contact me? All this time? I didn't know what to think. I thought maybe you were dead. How could you do this to me?" They were talking alone, outside, behind the building. The level of violence in the county had gone down drastically since election night. The subjugation of women was now done quietly, and the women were entirely hidden from sight. The Riders were still abusing women, but it was technically illegal now, and they usually did it only when they had Ezekial's permission. Ezekial turned a blind eye to what the Riders did to their captive women, and he relied on the Riders to punish the recalcitrant ones. To keep up the façade of religious justification for their actions, the Riders had branded the woman in the Penance video with a cross.

"Dad, let's keep it a secret between us – how Roland got shot."

"Stacey, I'm not ashamed of anything I did."

"Still, you don't want to be indicted. Not in this county."

He seemed to shrink back from her lawyer talk.

"Are you ever coming home for good, Dad? I think Mom would let you."

"Let's work on freeing Ruth's sister for now."

* * * * * *

Eleni made an appointment to move all her things out of Grant's apartment. She had told him she was planning a career representing international relief agencies, but he hadn't realized how many books on the current international situation she was reading, how many notebooks she had filled with articles and contacts, until he had to go find a bigger box to put it all in. It was amazing to him that such a first-rate, workaholic lawyer had so much energy left over to worry about the downtrodden of the world. She helped him load the boxes. He started to say how much he would miss their nights together, but he stopped himself. She knew that anyway. It went without saying they were both going to suffer a lot.

She put the last box in her car and came up to the apartment for one last glass of water. "So, Grant, what are the plans? Are you moving to Kansas, or is she moving here?"

"Um, I don't know. There aren't any arrangements."

"You two haven't decided?"

"There's no *two*. There's just me, so far."

"Oh." Eleni's jaw dropped. He had dumped her just on the chance he could get back together with Stacey.

"This is just something I have to do, Eleni. Go after her. If some day you see me in the gutter, or in an alcoholic ward, you'll know it didn't work out. But I have to try."

"Don't sell yourself short, Grant. Your belief in me – it really helped me. It still does. You're a good man, and they're hard to find."

At work, they both found themselves avoiding the conference room they'd held their trysts in. They kept their relations there just as professional as always, but the undercurrent was different. It was harder holding back sorrow than holding back joy. Eleni had circles under her eyes and obviously wasn't sleeping well. Grant was holding onto a glimmer of hope for some kind of better life with Stacey someday. It would have been more comforting if he had any idea what exactly that life would look like.

When he arrived at work about two weeks later, Jeanine Atwood, the office manager, told him at the door that Eleni was gone. She'd quit without telling him. Maybe that was for the best, but he hadn't counted on her disappearing so soon. Right away he asked Jeanine to put out some feelers for a new legal assistant. "We'll never find anybody like her again," Jeanine contributed. This made Grant feel even worse.

Two weeks later, the lawsuit came. She sued the company, and Amos individually, for creating a hostile workplace environment. The lawsuit alleged that Amos had encouraged her to engage in a highly sexual, highly emotional affair with her supervisor and had even provided a "secret location, on the work premises, for the conduct of intimate sexual relations between supervisor and subordinate employee during the work day." Such conduct led to "inappropriate sexual and emotional bonding between the subordinate employee and the supervisor such that employee's work could not be objectively evaluated by the supervisor" with the result that "employee's work history is marred by having held a position for which her work evaluations, and any future references based upon the quality of work for said company, are worthless." The lawsuit went on to claim that in the highly competitive field of international law, a worthless reference was worse than a gap in employment and would do substantial and permanent damage to her career.

"What the hell is this?" Amos waved the papers over Grant's desk. "I thought you two were getting along great."

"We broke up two weeks before she quit."

"You're kidding me. I couldn't tell you two were acting any different."

"That's because Eleni and I both know how to act like professionals."

"Huh. A lot of good that does me. Between me and the company, we're on the hook for ten million dollars. If she wins this case, we might as well kiss our business goodbye. Get right on it, okay?" He laid the papers gently down on Grant's desk.

"I can't, Amos."

"What?" Amos raised his hands dramatically and walked around the office in a tight circle. "What are you telling me now?"

"I'm the only real witness for the company, and for you. I can't be the lawyer and a witness in the same case. We'll have to hire outside counsel."

"What? Hire an outside lawyer? *Cha-ching*. This is already costing me money. I knew she was too good to be true. I swear I'm only hiring ugly bitches from now on."

*** ***

He got Eleni on the phone that night. "I thought it was fair and square," he started. "I didn't treat you any differently on the job, not before and not after we broke up."

"That's why I didn't sue you."

"Yeah, but … the company. And Amos. Do you think it's fair to sue them?"

"I'm alone now, Grant. My career means all the more to me now. I think I have a case. Amos led me on into a compromising situation. Now, if I put you or Amos as a reference, I'll be a laughingstock. I'll be the law student who slept her way into the good graces of the counsel for a raunchy tech startup."

"But nobody knew. Nobody had to know. Until you sued.

You're the one who revealed it."

"It would have come out anyway." Her voice was suddenly strained. She obviously knew this was the weak point in her argument.

He decided to let it go. He had hurt her badly. So what if she had one weak point in her argument. He had a weaker point in his whole life plan.

Chapter 29

"I need to warn you, Ruth. Ziba definitely told her husband about you." Sheila was obviously worried, or she wouldn't have risked detouring from her morning duties carting barrels across the lot. They met deep inside the chiller, between two rows of hanging carcasses. The line hadn't started yet for the day. The Greek had promised Ruth he would flash the lights in the chiller if anyone else came in early.

"Okay. We gotta get out of here fast."

"It might be too late. Ziba's husband said he was going to call Ezekial last night. And now there's this huge motorcycle guy in the parking lot. He's looking around. He didn't go into the offices, so he's not here on business. He's a Genesis Rider, I think."

"Is he carrying a gun?"

"Doesn't look like it. He's looking in the side door. I think he's waiting for the lights to go on in the boning room area. Ziba told her husband you worked there."

The large plant had only one security guard, and his main job was to guard the plant at night. There was rarely any security on the premises in the daytime. Stacey told Sheila to go out the outside door of the chiller, roll her barrel of offal to the dumping room and wait in her truck in the parking lot right behind it. "But stay out of that Rider's line of sight."

Ruth then opened the opposite door of the chiller and ran past the boning area toward the locker room to get her gun. But two other early bird workers were already in the locker room, and the lights to the whole boning area went on before she could wait them out. She ran back to her station on the line. She glanced frantically at the Greek's office as she passed. He saw her look and came out as she took her position. Nothing was moving yet, but she motioned for him to start the conveyor belt. With her helmet pushed down low to hide her face, she pulled her knife and did the work of two pullers, slashing off fat and separating shoulders as fast as a ten-year veteran. One of the other clod pullers who had been loafing up to the line jumped to work, too. The line of carcasses was moving slowly; the two of them could probably keep up until the rest of the pullers showed up.

The blood drained out of her face as she saw the large, muscled, tattooed body of a man turn the corner. She recognized the slit eyes, the round cheeks, the thick moustache of Hunter. He was the Rider who had kidnapped her and driven her to Reverend Ezekial's house to become his concubine. She remembered Ezekial's weak smile when they arrived at his house. She remembered Hunter's smirk when Ezekial, looking back over his shoulder to see if his wife was watching, asked him to chain Ruth up in the cabana behind the pool. Ruth had not seen Hunter since she was first taken. She could only hope he wouldn't recognize her.

Hunter clearly didn't expect her to be one of the clod pullers standing in their slickers and helmets right next to the line. He went right into the office instead. Ruth could hear the Greek yell for him to get out; then she heard the men struggling. Hunter came out alone after just a minute. He stood in place and looked around. There weren't any other offices in the area. He started slowly walking up the line, staring at each of the workers. It was too late to run, so Ruth tried making herself small.

It didn't work. "Hey!" He reached in between two moving carcasses and pushed her shoulder. "You're a woman underneath that raincoat, right?"

She expertly sliced off the shoulder of a carcass and dropped it on the moving belt. She was wearing her dark wig, which was covered by a yellow plastic helmet. A bloodstained slicker covered the rest of her body. He definitely couldn't know for sure who she was.

"What's your name?"

"What's it to you?"

"Is there a problem here?" The Greek suddenly showed up and stepped between them. "Get out, sir. I've already called security."

"Get away." Hunter backhanded him to the floor.

"What's your problem?" Ruth shouted. She noticed another worker start moving toward them. The line kept moving and the carcasses started to back up. "I've got work to do."

"You're messing with the Reverend's women. I'm here to beat that out of you. And I'm gonna have a *good* time doing it."

Ruth suddenly held the point of her knife to his chest and stared into his eyes. "In twenty seconds, I can have your heart out and beating its way down this conveyor belt."

"I'll take the liver and kidneys. Ought to take about five seconds for them." Her co-worker had come up from behind.

She pushed him back from the line with her knife point while her co-worker searched him for weapons. "Just a hunting knife. Six inches. Dull, worthless piece of crap." He threw the knife in the trash. "Get your ass out of here."

Ruth followed him to the door, keeping the point of her knife right at his spine. Then she turned back. Her legs started trembling as the fear sank in. She was worried about the Greek, but she found herself hugging her co-worker. "Oh my God. I don't even know your name. Oh my God. Thank you." She found herself crying. Her helmet fell off and the wig slipped halfway off her head. "We got to go help the Greek."

"Name's Howard, by the way."

*** ***

"Oh God, Mara." Renee collapsed on the bed next to her

only friend in Bible Land. "I feel so dirty."

"You've been with him all night?"

"Oh, no. He didn't pretend to like me. I was supposed to worship him. I guess I wasn't convincing enough."

"Did he hit you?"

"No. When I left the Rev's bedroom, he sent me to work in the nursery right after. I was just numb at first. I was watching the kids, but like a robot. Then this like, giant flood of anger started like, filling me up. It was like this fire burning from the inside. To tell the truth, I felt like killing his children then."

"Don't take it out on the children."

"Oh Mara, I slapped one of the little boys who was mouthing off!"

"Jesus, Renee!"

"It's awful, I know. I made it up to him. Tried, anyway. I couldn't stop it."

"Was the kid hurt?"

"No. No. We were playing together after that. Laughing and playing by the end. It was like the fire went out. But now I'm numb again. And I feel so dirty."

"Lie down next to me. Let me rub your back. You'll be fine."

Mara's hands felt good. Renee relaxed and tried not to hold back her black thoughts. "They didn't even give me a chance to like, wash. Who knows where that dick of his has been? He could have a million diseases."

Mara's hands on Renee's back went still. Her voice went flat. "He's been mostly with me."

"Oh. I didn't mean *that*. I didn't mean you."

"I never had a disease."

Renee rolled to her side and sat up. "Please don't be mad. You're my only friend in the world now." Renee could feel the numbness falling away again, feel her rage coming to the surface and dissolving into tears. She was afraid this was the cycle she'd be going through for the rest of her life. Mara wiped her tears with the edge of the sheet. Renee cried even more at that gesture of kindness, but then laughed at herself for that reaction.

"I am so, so lonely," she admitted. "I didn't know there were places like this, where you are not really a person, where you just don't matter." She started sobbing again.

"You matter to me." Mara insisted. "Hey, stop crying. We'll get through this."

Renee eventually started to breathe normally. "Mara, you've been through so much more than me. Tell me about yourself."

"Like, what?"

"You do have a boyfriend, right?"

"I do. He came along after Jimbo was born."

"Did you meet him in the bar?"

"He owns the bar. I mean, a different bar. I met him in the hospital. His wife was dying of cancer. He heard there was a newborn in the hospital that morning, and he came down to see the baby. His wife was dying. He said he just wanted to see a new baby who had just come into the world. We started talking."

"His wife …?"

"Died that afternoon. He came again and held Jimbo for a long time, walked up and down the hall holding him in his arms. It made me cry."

"Oh."

"He wanted to get married, but I kept putting him off. He's kinda old, like thirty-five or something. But he loves Jimbo."

"Maybe he'll find you."

"I can't count on that. Nobody knows where I'm at."

Renee sat up. "I've got to get out of here. I've got to escape. We'll be here *forever*, hidden from everybody we know, if we don't get out."

Mara was lying flat on her back, staring up at the darkened ceiling. "Don't try it, Renee. Don't try it. They'll catch you and send you to Penance. You see what happened to Dina. It's better to be a slave than a zombie."

Chapter 30

"You know Ruth is working at that processing plant. Now Ezekial found out about her. I mean, he knows there's a strange woman working at that plant who's part of the resistance, but he doesn't know it's her – yet."

"She's got to get out of there!"

"She's committed to saving another woman who works there. The woman and her little boy. They're both ready to escape. But Don keeps telling that her going too early might mess up some plan he has for rescuing Renee from Bible Land."

This wasn't the conversation Grant expected to have when he called Stacey for the first time after breaking up with Eleni. He was concerned about Ruth, whom he had taken under his wing during the election campaign. He had showed her there was a wider world than the one she had learned of from her father and Reverend Ezekial. He wasn't surprised that Ruth boldly took a job in the heart of Neola County in the hopes of finding her sister. He was worried about her safety now. But this conversation with Stacey was supposed to be about their romance, and if it could be started again.

"Is there anything I can do," he asked reflexively, "to convince Ruth to get out of that plant, now?"

As soon as he asked the question, he realized this was the right way to get to talk to Stacey. Stacey was not some isolated person on an island of emotional needs and wants. She was out in the world, dealing with it. The way to get to her was to be out there in the world with her.

"I can come to Kansas," he added.

"I don't think Eleni would like that."

"That's what I called you about. I broke up with her."

There was a long pause during which he waited for some

kind of sarcastic remark about his ex. It didn't come. "You said you'd never live in Kansas."

"I don't know where I can live. But I want to help you, and you're in Kansas."

"I miss you. Why don't you come visit me, for starters?"

"I will, soon." His tone was suddenly more tentative. "My job, um, it's not so loosey-goosey as it used to be."

"I know Amos gave you a lot of time off during the election campaign."

"Yeah, uh, I'm not exactly in the doghouse, but things are a little tighter now." She waited for him to go on. "Okay, I'll tell you. Eleni sued the company, and Amos, too. He's not too happy about that."

"Sued? What for?"

"Employment discrimination on the basis of sex."

"Oh. What does that mean? You gave her preferential treatment in return for her screwing you? Or you treated her like shit once you broke up with her? Or both?"

His response was curt. "That's an insult, Stacey, you know me better than that." He waited for a response from her. If she didn't believe in his integrity, there was no sense in going on with her.

"Okay," she sighed.

"Okay what?"

"I mean okay, I'm sorry I said that. I don't believe you would ever do anything sleazy like that."

He calmed down to explain the situation. "The lawsuit doesn't say anything about preferential treatment or harassment on the job. It says now that our past affair is public, any future references she gets from the company will be worthless, because people will assume any good reports the company provides will be the result of her having had a past sexual affair with me. And that will hurt her career."

"Oh, give me a break! Don't tell me that's a viable lawsuit

in Massachusetts."

"Our lawyer says it is. The Consent To Sex forms and the PR-26 forms aren't enough any more. There's one more form they've come up with for our situation, the RDR, or Recognition of Diluted Reference forms. Unfortunately, the RDR forms are new, and we didn't get her to sign one of those."

"So Eleni still has her claws in you."

"No. No. Our lawyer says it's a standard thing. A lot of women bring these cases. Men, too. Two hundred fifty thou is the standard settlement. I think Amos will pay, and we'll be through with her." But he hadn't called her to talk about Eleni. "You've done so much, Stacey, so quickly. The branding laws are gone, MOMS and MOMS-2 were defeated. I don't know how you did it. Just get rid of Conception Control and you can come visit me in Boston."

"I got some lucky breaks. But honestly, I think my career has already peaked. I am keeping up with my legal internship in case they ever let women become lawyers again here. But I honestly don't know what I'm going to do for money."

"Don't worry about money."

* * *   * * *

"You trust me, don't you, Dad?" Damien had never spoken to his father like that before. His assumption had always been that his father looked down on him because he didn't go to college, refused to work in the family business, and failed to set out on some definite career path of his own. All of those facts were true, but Damien always thought he detected admiration on his father's part for his independence, his creativity and the fact that he was (almost) supporting himself. In any case, his father had never treated him as dishonest, or stupid.

"The Greek tells me that woman you recommended for the clod puller job is working out great. You're a good judge of character, son."

Damien thought that was a strange thing to say. He filed his father's comment away to think about later. There were more important issues right now. "This is actually about her, Dad. A guy came after her yesterday. He had a knife. She and Howard had sharper knives, and they scared him off. But word is he's coming back tomorrow with his entire motorcycle gang."

"What's it all about?"

"I think it's this Genesis Riders stuff, kidnapping women and all that."

"Not in my plant! What does she need? More security?"

"I think that would help."

"You got it."

*** ***

The plans were in place. Don had figured out a way to get around the fortifications at Bible Land and rescue Renee, and he told the group gathered at Damien's record store that he needed just one more day to scout out the escape route. But they told him they couldn't wait that long.

"We don't have one more day. They're coming after Ruth tomorrow at the packing plant," Damien interrupted. "Dirk, my roommate, told me about it. I told you, he actually is a Genesis Rider himself. He should know. They're talking about sending over five to ten guys." Damien met their eyes, one by one. "My Dad's putting on extra security, but if you've seen our security company ...."

"Okay. Good info, Damien." Don turned to Ruth. "So, don't go back there, Ruth. You've gotten enough information already."

"I *am* going back. I promised Sheila. She's already been ratted out. They'll put her in Penance if I don't get her out tomorrow."

"Don't be a hardhead. I won't be ready to move on my

plan by tomorrow."

"I'm going tomorrow."

"I think you're both hardheads," Amy shouted over them. Damien blinked hard, and Don and Ruth were silenced for the moment. "If you have to get your friend Sheila out tomorrow, we'll just have to speed up the plan to rescue Renee. It might be a little harder, but have to do both." Don's look showed he wasn't used to taking the lead from his younger daughter. But Amy didn't flinch. "We have to, Dad."

Don turned toward Ruth. "Are you sure you can get Sheila and her boy out of there tomorrow?"

Ruth shrugged.

Don hesitated. Then he smiled. "Okay. If we're all in, let's go tomorrow."

"Oh, one more thing?" Damien had stepped back from the argument between Don and the two women. "Can I show Dirk the video of that woman going through Penance?"

"Are you crazy?" the conspirators all exclaimed together.

"Damien, don't you realize that would blow up our entire plan?" Don patiently explained. "Why would you even think of doing that?"

Damien backed up a step. "I don't know. He seems like a nice guy. I don't think he knows all what he's getting into."

Amy rolled her eyes. Ruth shook her head. Don, playing the paternal role, was more accepting. "Damien, we could try to convert Dirk. Maybe sometime in the future, but not until we have saved Renee and Sheila. It would be just too dangerous to put our trust in anybody connected with the Riders right now."

Chapter 31

Ezekial made no mention to Renee of their encounter in bed the night before. He treated her no differently than on any other day. Renee was surprised at her own reaction to this. She would have been disgusted if he leered or flirted, and she would have felt humiliated if he now treated her with any extra measure of consideration or respect – but there was absolutely no difference in his tone. She was just completely invisible to him. Somehow, this was almost worse.

She tried to get into the mind of this man who was certain that he was the sole instrument of God's power and wisdom on earth. She knew from his sermons that he had grown up as an only child. He said he had a blessed early childhood – but then Satan had slowly and insidiously befouled his family. His mother had stood by while his father defiled himself with a temptress. God revealed to the young Ezekial that the beautiful long-haired temptress was actually the devil in disguise. He had even tried to strangle her with his own eleven-year-old hands, but his father had pulled him off, the red sparks of hellfire glowing in his eyes. Ezekial learned then that the devil could not be bargained with, could not be beaten back with halfway measures. Those enslaved by the devil must be confronted and crushed.

But then Ezekial himself had been tempted by the wiles of Satan, whose enticements were stronger than his childish soul had ever imagined. He had fallen into sin. Even his mother could not beat the sin out of him. One afternoon he ran from home, ran across the fields for hours, into the wilderness, Satan's tentacles scratching, drawing blood, claiming his body, his soul. He despaired. He ran from God. He cursed God. Then God struck him down, and he was lost to the world. Then God brought him back, awakened him, spoke to him as he lay prostrate in a cold, muddy, stubbly wheat field, shivering with fear.

You are my messenger, my chosen one.

No. I am a sinner.

You are chosen. You cannot sin. You cannot doubt. You shall not submit yourself to the small judgment of men.

Renee realized that Ezekial had created with his fundamentalist frenzy an invisible shield that could not be argued with, or even fully understood, by any other person. He had put himself in a category of one, one who could not be measured or judged by any yardstick, because he was the yardstick. And he sold images of that yardstick to tens of thousands of followers; and they gave him their money, proving to himself that he alone channeled God's words. And those words warned him constantly about those minions of Satan who put man's welfare above God, those disciples of decadence who destroy families with drink, those temptresses whose artful cunning sets snares for God-fearing men everywhere.

"Isn't there anything, a suicide pill or something, that I can take?" Renee was in the bed with Mara.

"You know better. All pills are screened. Ever since Abigail offed herself."

"Offed herself? You never told me!"

"We're forbidden to mention even her name. You could never do that anyway. Not while you're carrying your baby."

"I don't want my baby raised here. I've got to get out of here."

"Please don't try to escape, Renee." Mara pulled her to her, stroked her long red hair, flattening it against her pale face. "Please don't try. Please. They'll catch you. They'll break you."

* * * * * *

The alarm bells woke everyone in Ezekial's house in Bible Land. Bright emergency lights snapped on in the hallways and in the ceilings of the wives' bedrooms. Dina's voice could be heard over the PA system, screeching the words. "Escape! Escape!"

Mara woke up confused and blinded by the lights. Then, in a flash of panic, she checked for Renee. She breathed a big sigh of relief to see Renee still lying beside her, her red hair now mussed and glowing like a gauzy fireball in the glare of the lights. Renee awoke slowly even in these conditions. "What's going on?"

"Somebody is trying to escape. I'm so glad it wasn't you."

The door opened and Ezekial walked in wearing only his pajamas. Joan followed close behind in a dressing gown. "The sensors caught someone in wives' garb trying to climb the fence," Joan explained. It wasn't clear who she was explaining this to. She stepped toward the wall where the wives were allowed to hang their garb on wooden pegs. She ran her hand across the garments as if searching for something. Then she turned toward the two women on the bed.

"Something's missing. Show us what's under the bed," she suddenly commanded the two puzzled women.

Renee reached under the bed and felt something there she hadn't expected. She pulled out a wife's robe and shoes. The shoes had mud on them. They couldn't be hers. She hadn't been outside in weeks. The robe was also dirty and, upon closer inspection, had a series of small tears across the front.

"Those are yours?" Joan commanded. It wasn't really a question.

"No. Mine are on the pegs, right next to …." But there was only one set of women's clothing on the pegs.

"Those clothes are Tamar's. They're her size," Joan declared, her voice now more hostile than ever. "So, it was *you* the surveillance cameras caught trying to climb the fence. The mud. The tears in your robe from the barbed wire. Follow me. All the wives must see you face justice."

"No! Won't you listen. You've always been fair to me, Joan."

It took all five other wives to drag her to the prayer and assembly room and hold her down.

"I'll call for backup," Ezekial announced as soon as Renee was solidly pinned to the floor.

"Please. Please. I didn't do anything. I was asleep in bed. You can ask Mara. I would never try to escape. I would never do anything to displease you."

Mara separated herself from the four other wives who held Renee down. She looked up as if she were about to speak.

"Mara," Joan commanded from behind clenched teeth as she held all her weight down on Renee's right leg, "have the common sense not to say anything right now."

Mara said nothing. And the evidence against Renee was strong. The camera had recorded a woman in wives' garb trying to climb the fence, to the point of catching her robe on some of the barbed wire at the top. Renee's robe, dirty and torn, hidden under her bed, was all the evidence needed for this one-man ecclesiastical court.

"Resist all you want now," Joan said, with a look of satisfaction on her face. "You're being sent to Penance. When you come back, you will be begging to fulfill the Reverend's every wish." She looked at the other wives. "Right, ladies?"

"Yes, Ma'am."

Ezekial came back into the room. Renee twisted herself from their grasp enough so she could face him. "Help me. It wasn't me, honestly. I'll do whatever you say."

"Oh, no," he said very calmly, pointing with his trembling finger at her like a superannuated teacher scolding a first grader. "Penance it is."

"I hope all your seed rots, you dirty old man."

Joan smacked her hard, then had the other women hold her up while she smacked her again. Joan ordered her dragged out to the front portico, where they zip tied her wrists together behind her to one of the pillars. Joan smacked her in the face one last time. Ezekial didn't participate. He didn't even give any specific orders. The women seemed eager to show they knew what to do on their own. Once she was bound to the pillar, they left Dina there to watch her until the Genesis Rider would arrive to take her away to Penance. Renee tried to catch Dina's eye, hoping to ask for some kind of mercy. She begged Dina to set her free, but Dina ignored her pleas.

Chapter 32

Renee was relieved that the Rider who came to transport her to Penance was not Hunter himself. Hunter was the Rider who had taken her sister Ruth from their father's home. The last time she'd seen Ruth, she was being tied to the back of his motorcycle, screaming that her legs were being burned.

There was no resisting this new Rider. He unclipped her hands from behind the pole and, twisting her arm behind her back to maintain complete control, he marched her over to his cycle and zip tied her wrists together in front of her and to the strap on the seat. He was actually quite skinny, but he was strong enough to make any resistance futile. She searched for something to say.

"My sister got burned on one of these cycles," she offered.

"Not necessary. Put your feet on these pegs. Looks like somebody already slapped you up pretty bad."

"A woman did," she said, suddenly dejected at the thought. "They say it's worse in Penance."

"I wouldn't know," he said, pressing the starter button on his engine. As soon as the engine caught, it drowned out any further conversation.

The orange sunrise slid over the sorghum fields which had faded to brown in the weeks since Renee had been taken to Bible Land. The stark autumnal landscape suited her mood; she imagined the land was saving its green fertility for other people, free people. Just being on the road, moving fast between the fields, was a piquant reminder of the freedom she had lost. After about fifteen minutes he stopped for gas at a self-service station outside of a small town. There was a man just getting into his truck as they pulled in. She tried to scream for help, but the Rider just revved his motor and waved as the truck driver drove off, waving back a friendly

Kansas good morning.

"Don't do that again. You don't know how much trouble I'll be in if I don't deliver you."

"You're taking me to be tortured."

"I never heard anything about that."

"So, you don't know anything. What are you, then? Just an Uber driver?" Renee knew she had absolutely nothing to lose.

He revved the engine and pulled out of the station. Twenty minutes later, she felt the engine stumble once, then twice, then cut out completely. He guided the silent cycle to a stop on the dusty shoulder of the road. Across the fence bordering the road was another dying field. He took off his helmet. She was surprised at the anxiety in his face. "What's wrong?"

"Keep your mouth shut. And get off the seat."

"Did you forget that you have me tied down to the seat strap?"

"Shut your mouth!" He searched for another zip tie, then bound both of her wrists together again, then cut the original tie holding her to the seat strap. "Now get off."

Getting off wasn't easy. Her wrists were still tied together, and she was wearing the cumbersome concubine dress.

"Get off the seat. Hurry up."

"What? You can't fix it? We're going to walk now?"

"Shut up!" But his eyes looked more worried than angry. "Battery cables are loose. I need to get under the seat to tighten them."

"If you knew they were loose, why didn't you fix them before you left? How stupid can you be?" She didn't care if she got him mad. She didn't care if he hit her. She had nothing to lose.

"Shut up."

She was off the bike by then. He stared at her, shifting his weight from one foot to the other. "Get up near the front. Put your wrists on the handlebars."

"You're afraid I can outrun you in this dress? With my hands tied together?" she mocked him. But she did as she was told. He put his hands up as he approached her – to tie her wrists to the cycle, she assumed. But instead, he reached into a leather pouch attached to the handlebars.

"Fuck! Fuck! Fuck!"

"Is that supposed to be a tool kit? All you've got in there is a pair of pliers."

Breathing hard, he looked her in the eyes for the first time. "I can do it with these. It's going to take longer, though."

"I'm in no hurry to be tortured."

"I don't know anything about that." He pulled the pliers out of the bag, then shrugged. "But I'll make you a deal, lady. I won't tie you to the handlebars while I'm fixing it, if you promise to keep your mouth shut."

*** ***

Don had been sleeping lately in the back of the abandoned machine shop in Neola County where, during the election, he had manufactured fake ankle bracelets and other devices to defeat the pervasive government surveillance. As a branded addict with no right to drive, he kept out of sight during the daylight hours. He drove his practically invisible electric motorcycle only at night. He had saved his son from being jailed on a Feto-Terrorism charge, and he had saved Stacey's life – twice. He was listed as a person of interest in the killing of Roland Asher, but he had not been indicted because there was no actual evidence against him.

After working on his plans all night, he was about to lie down for his sunrise nap on the bed he had welded out of old angle iron when he got the call he had been waiting for on his burner phone.

"She's gone. She's out of Bible Land now. A Rider is taking her to Penance right now. They left five minutes ago. This had better work."

It was Joan. After a couple of Sunday after-services conversations, Don had become convinced that Joan hated the concubine system. But he couldn't convince her to do anything about it until he took the step of showing her the Penance video on his phone. She said she had seen Dina sent to Penance, but she had assumed it was just some sort of psychological indoctrination. When she saw the real thing, she turned away and gagged. When she recovered, she sat back on the bench beside him, her back straight, in utter silence. Don's gaze was patient but persistent. He just waited. This would have to be her decision. "This is too much," she finally said, her voice edged with resolution. "This is not God's work. Just tell me what I can do."

It was Joan who had been out at the fence around Bible Land the night before, deliberately tearing a wife's robe on the barbed wire and making sure the knees were covered in dirt, then planting it under Renee's bed. The only way they could get Renee out of Bible Land was to have her sent to Penance. The plan was for Don to drive Damien to the Riders' headquarters on the night that Renee was to be taken there. Damien would then unlock the electronic locks and set her free. They would bring bolt cutters in case she was chained. That was the plan, except the rescue was supposed to take place at night, under cover of darkness.

"Sorry," Joan had apologized to Don on her burner phone. "I had to wait until everyone was asleep. There was a child crying almost all night and a wife minding it. I couldn't get started until it was almost dawn."

"I think I can do it anyway. The Riders aren't known for being early risers."

"But wait, Don. I've only got a minute. Afterwards, Renee's roommate, Mara, attacked me, I mean physically attacked me, when we were alone in her room. She was choking me. I had to tell her I was on her side, and that Renee being taken was part of the plan."

"Oh, shit."

"No, I convinced her I'm on her side, too. I think it's okay. But listen. This seems important. Mara told me that Renee saw a book in Ezekial's office. It had the names and locations of all the taken women. If we can get that book, and get the police, or somebody ...."

"Oh my God! That is great! Get it!"

"Easy for you to say. I don't even know where it is yet."

"Find it! And I'll get Amy on the case."

Amy had been working with Don on this part of the plan, pretending to be Don's wife instead of his daughter. Fortunately, the congregation in Ezekial's church was used to child brides and had paid little attention to their age difference. Once Don was convinced that Joan was on their side, he had revealed to her who Amy really was. Joan had laughed. She was impressed that Amy was the sister of the famous Stacey Davenport. She was awed that Amy would show herself in Neola County and risk being taken herself. Amy had just nodded then, no longer surprised at people taking her seriously.

Her father's call woke Amy up as she slept on the sofa bed in her aunt's house. This was her only home since her mother's house had been burned down the night of the election. She was fifteen and not used to waking up early. Her father explained the importance of the book that Ezekial had in his house in Bible Land.

"You want me to get it, right?"

"It's a lot to ask, honey. If you get caught in Neola County ...."

"Yeah. Yeah. How do I get there? Ruth already took the truck to go to work at the processing plant."

"I know. Ruth is making her move today, too. We're running short of people. That's the only reason I'd ask you to do this. Here's what you need to do. Steal your mother's car. Keep off your phone once you've crossed the county line. When you're on your way, I'll call Joan."

"Then what?"

"Drive to Bible Land. You know the way. We've been there before in the dark. Joan's inside. She's totally on our side now, and she knows you. Stay hidden outside. She'll figure some way to get it out to you."

"Why doesn't she just make a pdf of it and email it to me?"

"Ezekial's women are forbidden to use computers or cell phones. Only the man himself knows the passwords. Her only phone is a secret burner. Don't call her. Just wait for her to call."

Amy called her mother and told her she was taking her car, just to keep her from calling the police. Her mother was resigned by this time to the fact that she had not one but two headstrong daughters. She didn't bother to lecture her that she was still only fifteen years old and didn't have a license. She suspected her daughter was going into dangerous territory in Neola Count, but she knew her opinion wouldn't have any effect on her. She had gained some faith in the past few months that Don was as quick and cunning as their enemies. And she had actually gained some faith in Amy, too.

* * * * * *

Damien had already installed battery-operated digital locks on the Riders' clubhouse as well as on a little white shed they called Penance. Each lock worked only when the proper code was punched in. When installing the locks, Damien had made a big deal of turning his head and not looking when Hunter, the chief Rider, put in the code for the gang. But what

Damien didn't tell them was that each lock had an alternate code, known only to himself and Don. Don and Damien could thus enter either of these places whenever they wanted.

The plan had been simple. Arrange for Renee to be caught and delivered in the middle of the night, then punch in the alternate code to silence the alarm, then unlock the door to Penance and free her. They knew from Damien's previous visit to Penance exactly what size bolt cutters they would need to free Renee. The only possible hitch was the off chance that the Rider who delivered her would want to start the punishment himself. That didn't seem likely. Hunter was the only one they had seen on the surveillance camera exacting penance so far. He wouldn't be getting up in the middle of the night. Whoever delivered Renee would probably be low on the totem pole and not allowed to have first crack at a captive. But, just in case, Don brought his crossbow.

The clubhouse was in a grey barn a hundred yards down a dirt road behind an old, boarded-up, peeling-white Victorian farmhouse. The shed was next to the barn. Their original plan had been to hide in the brush on the other side of the dirt road from the clubhouse and simply wait for Renee to be delivered in the dark. It was after sunrise now, but they still hoped no Riders would be hanging around. A minute after they turned off the main road, however, they spotted two Riders crouched in the dirt in a rectangle of shade in front of the clubhouse, working on one of their cycles. Don's heart jumped. Quickly, he weighed their chances of turning back unseen and unheard. Something like this might be possible, as his electric cycle was whisper quiet. But then his cycle caught the eye of one of the crouching Riders, who squinted at them, eyes shaded by his hand, and stood up.

"What'll we do?" Damien's voice quivered.

"Maybe they're just curious about the electric cycle. Let's go talk to them." Don turned his front wheel in their direction.

"No! They know me. Those two were here when I put in the security system. Let me talk to them." Damien jumped off the back of the electric cycle and walked quickly toward the two men. Don urged the cycle slowly along behind.

"What's up?" Damien shouted as he approached them. Don could hear the quiver in his voice. He hoped the two Riders couldn't. The Rider who had first noticed them, a bulky red-haired guy with a matching short moustache, stared right past Damien to the electric motorcycle, his mouth puckered in interest.

"What the hell kind of bike is that?"

"Made it myself. All electric. With part of an old Tesla battery," Don shouted.

"No headlight?"

"It's a work in progress."

"You a friend of the security installer here?"

"Yeah ...um, I brought him here." Don thought it was better to state the obvious than risk forging ahead with a lie. The redhead seemed satisfied. But the other guy – blonde hair, movie star chin – stepped out in front of Damien, who started trembling.

"The security alarm went off last night." Damien ad-libbed. "Anyway, that's what the company computer said. Sometimes the sensors in the field are set a little too sensitive. I just need to check the adjustments."

"You're saying you set it wrong?" Blondie looked past Damien to Don. "What are all those tools strapped to the side of your cycle? Why do you need bolt cutters to cut that teeny alarm wire? You guys are up to something."

"That's enough," Damien yelled to Don. He sprinted back. "Let's get going."

Don's cycle was facing the wrong direction, and he had to circle around. But the two Riders also had a ten-second delay while they both hopped on the one cycle they had working. The electric cycle sped off quickly, spraying dust behind, while the big Harley roared to life and started to catch up. Don made it off the dirt, and the Tesla torqued itself down the road and gained a little more separation. The Harley screamed after them.

Both cycles seemed to have about the same top speed. Don prayed the batteries would last until they reached safety in Cosgrove County. There was nothing he could do now to save Renee. Except …. He remembered the crossbow. He didn't doubt he could suddenly pull over, get out his weapon and skewer the two pursuing Riders. He'd killed three people with that crossbow, but only when each of those three people had been about to kill somebody else.

The pursuit had lasted about two miles so far. Don glanced down at his battery gauge. It was going down faster than he thought. He still thought he could make it to Cosgrove County. The sun still wasn't far up from the horizon. A sign indicated a crossroads a mile ahead. He decided to turn east to get the sun in his pursuers' eyes. A quarter mile after the turn, to slow them down further, Damien threw the bolt cutters down in the road. That plan worked better than they could have possibly hoped. The cutters bounced up spectacularly as the Riders approached. The Harley swerved to avoid the tool and almost went down. The cycle wobbled back and forth across the full width of the narrow road, then suddenly lurched to a stop.

Don tripled his lead, then stopped himself and looked back. He could tell that the Riders were unnerved, or tired, or maybe out of gas. He waited to see what they would do next. They stared at him and Damien as their motor gurgled and backfired. The chase clearly wasn't as much fun for them after their scare with the bolt cutters. They weren't willing to die to find out what Damien was up to. They sat on their

Harley and watched Don and Damien slip farther away. Even though they weren't going anywhere, they revved their Harley constantly, because that's what you did when you had a Harley. They didn't hear the other motorcycle carrying two people crossing behind them on the road that led back to the clubhouse.

Chapter 33

Amy tore down the straight, flat roads of Neola County at close to 100 miles an hour. She stopped the instant she could see the roof of the guard station of Bible Land, then backed into a footpath, her tires crunching back into the underbrush far enough for her to be out of sight of the road. But she had nothing to do then but wait. She wasn't supposed to call Joan. She knew the danger Joan would be in if she were caught. Amy had developed a bad habit. When she was nervous, she often found herself running her finger up and down over the brand on her forehead. She screamed at herself to stop it now. Then she held her breath, terrified that somebody had heard. It was a long, agonizing twenty minutes before her phone rang.

"Can't talk," Joan's voice crackled with fear. "Go to the guard station. Act calm. You are coming to pick up some food we prepared."

Amy did as she was told. It was more nerve-racking to walk up to the guard in plain sight than it had been to sneak around the fence in the dark. She wished she carried a gun like Ruth did. But she had to smile, act like the happy little puppy just bursting with joy to be helping Ezekail and his church. At the same time, she had to remember not to toss her hair, or even move her head around enough for her brand to show. She decided to act the shy, demure but inwardly ecstatic little acolyte.

She realized she was playing the role of herself at eight years old, when her family was together and happy and she knew if she was nice, she would earn all the affection and advantages her older sister Stacey had been given. She shyly informed the guard that she was sent from the Precious Blood congregation to pick up some food offerings that the wives of

Reverend Ezekial himself had prepared.

"Prepared for what?"

"The Holy Fall Festival." Amy suspected this was Ezekial's version of Halloween. She tried to act as if Holy Fall Festival had been around since the time of Jesus himself. "It's at our church this year!"

"Okay, honey. That's nice." The guard, a middle-aged man with swarthy skin and dark hair, smiled patronizingly at her. Perfect, she thought.

Dina struggled out with the packages. She started to list the separate food items, but Amy just grabbed everything from her. The guard helped her rearrange them into two larger boxes, then motioned for Dina to return to the house.

"Don't you need some help carrying these, honey?"

"Um." His offer was the one thing she was totally unprepared for. What could she say? She racked her brain for some appropriate explanation.

"Who brought you here, anyway?"

"Um, pastor says I must walk in Jesus's footsteps three thousand steps a day, carrying a burden as Jesus carried the cross. I have to do it alone, as Jesus did. But I'm not afraid. It's really an honor. Pastor's waiting for me at the crossroads."

The guard shook his head. Amy guessed he was a paid guard and not one of the converted. "Okay, honey. Hope the food don't get too cold."

Reaching the car, she looked back to make sure the guard wasn't following her. She hoped the book would be somewhere in the boxes, but she didn't have time to find it right then. She would just have to have faith. She crunched her car back onto the road and headed back to Cosgrove. But just as she crossed the county line she received a call from Stacey, who told her to head straight for Topeka instead.

*** ***

Stacey met Amy at the door to her legislative office in Topeka and helped her pile the boxes on her desk. Amy saw nothing inside but food. She felt a rush of panic that she had screwed up. But Stacey seemed to know what she was doing. Pushing the other containers roughly aside, she reached for the casserole dish. There was aluminum foil over the top, but Stacey put her fingers right through it, squished her fingers around – then dragged Ezekial's book up from the bottom. She held the book up with her two fingers dripping with casserole goop. The book was wrapped in plastic and also covered with goo. Martha left and came back with tissues from the little square box that was always sitting neatly on her desk while Amy ran back with paper towels from the women's room. The whole operation took place in Stacey's legislative office. They laid the little leather book on paper towels on Stacey's desk and unwound the plastic wrap inch by inch. They could soon see the book was still in perfect condition. Stacey wiped her own fingers with tissues so she could grab the book as soon as the last wrapping was cleared. They ran with it over to Martha's office where they all paged through it together.

"This is everything we hoped for," Stacey exclaimed. "Copy this quick! One for me, one for Golsch and one for Her Honor the governor. Then scan the whole thing." Stacey's excitement made her bossy. Angela, her aide, literally ran down the hall to the copy machine. "Go with her, Amy. Make sure no one snatches that book from her."

"Oh, my God, this is great! This list includes everything. All the women taken and how much they were bought for. Their real names matched up with their new biblical names. Where each one came from and where they are now. Their husbands' names. Even a list of who was sent to Penance, and when. We can match up those Penance dates with the video. Then we'll have proof of a real crime against a real person who has a real address the police can find."

"What about Ruth?" Amy asked. "Any word yet?"

"No word from Ruth yet. Her sister was taken to Penance today."

"Oh God! Have they started in on her? Is she on the surveillance video?"

"She's not at Penance yet. Dad and Damien were supposed to rescue her from there this morning, but they're not there either. Something went wrong. I don't know what."

Stacey called Toby Ratchenfeld, the governor's legislative liaison. "You know that video I gave you, of that woman being punished. Have you decided yet whether it's worth the governor's time to see it?"

"Video? Oh, yes, I remember that you gave me a video, but I haven't had time to look at it. I promise I'll get right on it tomorrow."

"We now have the name of that woman on that video, and the address where she's being held."

Ratchenfeld seemed less than excited. "Oh. That may be important. Do me a favor. Fax me that information and I'll have it available when I look at it … tomorrow."

Stacey hung up and called Golsch. She knew he could get in to see the governor any time he wanted. Golsch himself was always hard to reach, and Stacey was told he was out of town, in Washington, D.C. But Stacey knew she was one of the few people on earth he had an actual emotional bond with, and she might be able to get through to him. On her first try, though, she was told to leave a message.

"We still don't know what's happening in Neola County," Amy worried. "Renee's somewhere in that county on the back of a Rider's motorcycle. Ruth is still working at the processing plant. She refuses to get out of Neola without saving her friend, Sheila. They might be waiting their chance to escape. But Hunter knows where Ruth's working. I think he will definitely go after her today."

"What good does it do to keep saying that?" Stacey complained.

"Oh, that's right. Little sisters are supposed to be seen and not heard."

Stacey flinched at this blow from an unexpected quarter. "Oh. Amy, I'm so sorry. Do I come off like that?"

"Sometimes, yes, you do."

Chapter 34

The motorcycle ran for about ten miles before it stuttered to a stop again. "Battery cables?" Renee was mocking him still. "I guess you couldn't fix it good enough last time with your big pair of pliers." She knew they were a lot closer to Penance now. The fear that they would crush her spirit was sharper. But she decided to take it out on him while she still had any spark left. "You don't really know how to fix it, do you?"

"Will you shut up!"

He paced back and forth in the dust on the side of the road. Then he made her get off. This time he did attach her wrists to the handlebars. She could neither sit nor stand up straight. Her back started to hurt. But he managed to tighten the cables quickly, then tied her again to the seat. He stepped back.

Smirking, she turned her face up to his. "You're really pissed at me, aren't you? But I bet you won't hit me. You're not the type of guy who can hit a woman, are you?"

"Shut the fuck up!"

He started the motor again and they pulled off in a cloud of dust. It was another twenty minutes before they turned onto a dirt road next to an old, boarded up Victorian farmhouse, a dirt road that soon led to a barn with a little white shed off to the side. A shiver of fear silenced Renee. For a full minute she held her breath, waiting to be dragged off, trying not to imagine what would happen in the next few hours. Her Rider, off the motorcycle now and walking toward the clubhouse, turned and stared at her for a second. It seemed to her almost like he was waiting for her next taunt.

It didn't take long for the next taunt to come. Pulling up his carabiner to get his key as he approached the door, he suddenly stopped short. She could see what his problem was. He had a key, but there was no lock. A barn like that usually had a big padlock, but all this one had was a small touchscreen. He didn't turn around to face her. Swinging his carabiner on its strap in a slow circle, he slouched around the edge of the barn toward the little shed. Renee couldn't see what happened there, but when he came back in just a few seconds, she guessed. "They changed the locks on you, didn't they? And they didn't even give you the code."

"Shut up. You're right."

Renee realized her reprieve would be over as soon as any Genesis Rider with the code arrived at the clubhouse. She had to get out of the immediate area soon. "I got an idea. Why don't you take me to your place?"

"My place? It's a barn."

"This is a barn. Why don't you take me to your place? I could fix us something to eat."

"I don't give a shit about food."

"It's hot out here. We could get something to drink."

"Huh." He didn't really look like he was interested in eating or drinking.

"I promise I won't try to escape. You can keep me tied up there."

He didn't respond, but he came closer. He put his hand up to her face and stroked her cheek. "It would be fun to keep you around." Like a pet, Renee thought. But there was something gentle in his touch. She knew what she had to do.

"You don't have to rape me. I'll do it with you, nice." She leaned into his touch. She thought of Mara, degrading herself with Ezekial just so she could have a name close to her real name. Renee had just found out what she would do to keep herself out of Penance. He wanted her, she could tell. But he still hesitated.

"I can tell you're not one of the mean ones," she went on.

"I can't help liking you. Take me to your place. We deserve to be happy for a while."

*** ***

"There's no way we can stop them now from putting Renee in that shed." Don and Damien had arrived at the record store after their escape from the two Riders. Now Don slumped to the counter, his head in his hands, while they recharged the batteries to his motorcycle. "It's all my fault. It was a stupid plan, much too dangerous."

Damien didn't respond. He hadn't spoken since they were discovered by the two Riders outside the clubhouse. Don would have thought he was in shock, but Damien had demonstrated the good sense to throw the bolt cutters in the path of their pursuers and make their escape possible. Don had pulled out his crossbow then; but angry as he was, he realized in that moment that eliminating those two losers wouldn't help Renee one bit.

"There's nothing we can do to help her," he moaned.

Damien stared at him, disappointed. "I can think of one thing." His voice was thick, like he was pushing the words out. "The video. The minute she's there we can prove a crime is being committed. I'll put it on social media in real time. The police'll have to do something about it."

Now Don was energized. "I don't want thousands of people watching that!" He took a quick glance at the screen. "Son, if Renee gets punished and there's a video of it, nobody gets that video but Stacey. You hear?"

"Okay. Okay. But listen. You've got to stay here to charge your cycle's battery, right? I have to go. I going to take my car and clear out all my electronic equipment and move back into my father's house. You know Dirk is one of them, right? I'm not afraid of Dirk. He's really not a bad guy, but the Riders know where I live. They'll come after me. I gotta get out of there right now."

"That means I have to be the one to watch the video?"

"Buck up, old man. There's nothing happening on that video stream right now, and there might not ever be."

Chapter 35

When Damien arrived at his place, Dirk's motorcycle was parked beside the barn door. Damien had installed an electronic lock on their own barn too, and it seemed to be working, but the door wouldn't slide open. When he banged on it, he heard Dirk's voice inside. "Hang on!" The door opened a crack.

"What's all this?" Damien saw that Dirk had driven an old Brushhog against the door.

"Uh, I got somebody here, a girl."

"You dog! Nine o'clock in the morning!"

The main floor of the barn functioned as Damien's kitchen, living room and electronic shop, as well as Dirk's storage area for his tools for his day job and his supply of extra motorcycle parts. The beds were in the hayloft. Damien had built steps up to it. After Dirk moved in, they had shoved in place large pieces of plywood to make some semblance of two separate bedrooms – for occasions just such as this, Damien thought with a grin.

Damien saw the "girl" out of the corner of his eye as she filled a pitcher with water from the spigots that used to hang over the watering trough. She seemed to be walking very awkwardly. But Dirk grabbed his attention. "What is the code at the clubhouse, man? I was over there this morning and couldn't get in."

"I thought I gave you the code."

"If you did, I forgot it."

Damien thought he heard a sound from the woman at the sink. He looked her over for the first time. "Hey, she's dressed like all those wives in Ezekial's cult."

"Um, yeah, I got one of those."

"You bought her from the Genesis Riders? You own her?"

Dirk just nodded, avoiding Damien's eyes.

"Does that mean she's going to live here?"

"Man, I don't know! Just give me the code."

Damien was confused. The woman caught his eye as she stood facing him. Her brown garb was torn and dusty. Then, to Damien's astonishment, she lifted up her skirt almost to her knees. He saw why she was walking awkwardly. Dirk had hobbled her, tying her ankles close together with a short rope.

"Just give me the code, man, and we'll be out of here." Dirk was anxious.

"Wait a minute. Did you steal her?" Damien didn't know what he was getting into with Dirk, but he decided he couldn't just turn his back on the situation. The woman was a captive. Dirk was much stronger than him, but he couldn't afford to be afraid.

"No, man. It's legit. I bought her fair and square. Isn't that right, honey?"

Honey quickly nodded yes. Too quickly, Damien thought. The woman obviously was calculating that Dirk was still in control of the situation.

"She's one of those slaves? Can you make her do anything you want?"

"Hell, I don't know. Will you give me the goddam code?"

"No! We're friends, Dirk. And you need to see something first."

Damien practically shoved his phone in Dirk's face. Dirk smiled at first at the video of the woman tied down in Penance, but then his expression quickly changed, and he dropped his head. He refused to watch it to the end.

"That's where you're taking her, Dirk. Do you really want to do that?"

Dirk shook his head no without raising his eyes. "But, you know, I like her. Can I keep her here?"

The woman hobbled over to the table and spoke to Dirk. "I like you, too. But I have a boyfriend, and I'm pregnant with his child. We were supposed to have been married by now."

"Besides," Damien added, "Hunter would never let you keep her."

Dirk gritted his teeth and waggled his head vehemently. "I *knew* not to mess with women!"

"Oh, no," the woman sat down uninvited at the table. "You *should* mess with women. I mean mess with them in a good way. You're the kind of guy women like."

Damien looked at the woman closely for the first time. How could he have not noticed that red hair? How could he have not figured out the situation sooner? "You're Renee, right? He got you from Ezekial's."

Renee nodded. "He was taking me to Penance. I didn't do anything. I was framed."

"Do you want to get free of Ezekial?"

"Of course. Oh, please."

"Okay, let's go then. We have to leave right now. The only safe place is Cosgrove County. Your sister lives there. She's been looking for you for weeks."

"But my boyfriend is in Neola County."

"Right now, the only safe place for you is Cosgrove County. If you stay in this county, they'll pick you up again, and law enforcement here is in league with them. You'll be back worse than when you started today."

"I would never do that to you. Put you in that place." Dirk, shaking his head, his eyes looking down at the table, was still a few beats behind everybody else.

"Dirk, you should come, too. Hunter will be after you by this time tomorrow."

"I'll take him out with my .357 if he does."

"Just come with us for a few days. I think things are going

to get better," Damien assured him. *Unless they get worse*, he said to himself.

*** ***

He stood behind Ruth and pulled the gun out of her holster.

When Ruth jumped to confront him, the Greek was adamant. "No! I saw you bring it from your locker. I can't have that in here. We have four security officers in the parking lot. Those guys won't be allowed in."

Ruth got a ding on her phone from Sheila, who was playing lookout near the door to the offal dump, next to the parking lot. She rushed to the back door and looked out the tiny window. Four security guards were waving off seven or eight motorcycles that had entered the parking lot. Their marked security cars were parked bumper to bumper, blocking the pathway to the parking lot. They were armed, but their guns were not drawn.

The group got off their cycles and tried to rush the guards. The guards, as if they had been expecting this, moved in unison to grab the first person to make contact, bent him over, and handcuffed his hands behind his back. The two biggest guards held the other Riders at bay while this happened. The whole group of Riders seemed to forget everything but freeing their comrade. They pushed and shoved the guards and their captive back and forth, trying to free him. The officers pushed back, meanwhile moving their captive toward the security vehicle. The Riders frantically tried to free him, jamming the door shut so he could not be put inside. Finally, they overpowered the four guards and dragged their handcuffed friend away and back toward the road. But he was still handcuffed, and now the odds were only seven to four. The guards resumed their defensive position. There was no chance the Riders would try another outright assault on this batch of armed and determined security officers. It looked like it was going to be a pushing and shoving battle, and the guards were holding their own.

The boning room went suddenly dark around Ruth, and she could hear the ceiling chain screech to a halt. She reached out to feel for the carcasses to steady herself. But the fleshy shoulder she touched was not cold, and it was not that of an animal. She jumped just as the lights flashed back on to see Hunter standing right in front of her.

Ruth hopped over the now moving belt, knocking chunks of bloody meat off as she landed, slid, fell, dropped her knife, rolled off the belt and headed back up the boning line toward the chiller. Hunter followed behind with amazing quickness for such a bulky man. Further up the line, Howard, boning knife in hand, stuck his foot out behind and tripped him. The lights flashed off and on again.

Ruth turned and opened the door to the chiller and went inside, hoping to hide among the hanging carcasses. The light was always dim in the chiller. She pushed herself through three rows of hanging meat, keeping her feet apart for balance as the heavy bodies swung on their hooks. She was trying to make her way to the small door on the other side of the chiller which led to the parking lot outside. But then she heard the door from the boning room open, and she froze. The hooks started moving, and the carcasses started swaying, slowly slapping her as they continued their circuitous path through the chiller. Then the room went completely black.

She heard Hunter curse as he was struck by a cold carcass. She knew he must be disoriented. But then she saw the beam of a flashlight playing around the hooks near the ceiling.

"I'm ready for your shit this time." His strong baritone voice played around the cold carcasses.

The flashlight, and his voice, added new dimensions to her fear. But she knew he still couldn't actually see her through the multiple moving lines of carcasses. The low clanking of the machinery covered the sound of her breathing. She thought she could still make it to the back door by feel and find her way out. But then, he gradually lowered the light and played it around the floor. He had figured out that the carcasses were hung high and he should be able to see her from the knees down. He was crouching down to that level so he could find her. There seemed to be no doubt he would find her.

She jumped up and grabbed a hook and wrapped her legs around one of the carcasses. The beam of his flashlight passed below without spotting her. She shinnied up the slimy meat until she got the crook of an elbow over the hook. The light was moving around the floor, but it wouldn't spot her up high. But the line was still slowly moving, and she realized with a shot of fear that she was now being conveyed away from the outer door and back toward Hunter, who was still crouched down near the door she came in through.

She put all her hopes on the element of surprise. As her hook slowly circled, she saw him hovering near the floor, his balding head, massive shoulders and even larger belly out- lined faintly in the glow from his flashlight. She realized he didn't know there was another door. She wondered for a quick second if she could pass right over him without being seen and hang on until she got to that door. But right then he started to get up. He had almost straightened up by the time her hook swung near. She jacked her legs back, then forward, and kicked him in the face.

He was knocked flat, and she fell on top of him. He dropped the light, and she felt his massive body struggling under her. She panicked, knowing she had to get away before he got himself together and grabbed her. But he was disori- ented, and she easily pushed herself off him, got her feet on the ground and ran out the same door they both came in. The sudden light seared her eyes. She ran back up the line, away from the boning room, figuring she knew that area better than he did.

She ran along the moving line of freshly killed cattle that were skinned, cut in half, mounted on hooks and being conveyed toward the chiller. The human path alongside was safely railed and easy to follow. But soon she heard the chiller door behind her open and shut, and Hunter appeared not fifty feet behind her. She had no choice but to keep running upstream against the flow of carcasses being dragged toward the chiller. She quickly ducked around the massive blade that was chopping the hanging bodies in half. She gained ground there, and she was now dodging the dangling hoofs of the headless, skinless bodies waiting their turn at the blade. Then she hit a dead end.

The walkway for humans stopped ten feet in front of her. To her left and ten feet down, workers in raincoats and helmets and goggles were gutting the headless cattle and pulling out the offal into a large pit. The walkway for humans continued on the other side of the offal pit, but it was not connected to the walkway she was on. She couldn't believe she hadn't known this. She had to turn and face Hunter. He was taller than her, but this was not an advantage for him. He had to duck to be out of the way of the twitching carcasses still gliding by.

"Hey, look up there!" It was the oldest, stupidest, simplest trick in the book, but Hunter looked up – just in time to be kicked hard in the side of his head by a headless, skinless, bloodless bovine. He went down hard, and Ruth moved fast this time. She jumped around behind him, got between him and the wall and used her legs to push him off the walkway, under the still-kicking cattle hooves and into the offal pit. The workers in the pit looked up in surprise. Somebody sounded the horn to shut the line down. But Hunter did not give up. He quickly rolled over and started crawling back through the pit toward the walkway. Ruth ran back toward the boning room. When she reached the boning room, she saw Howard coming towards her. She stopped to catch her breath.

"Can you help me?" she gasped. "He got past security somehow. He's mad enough to kill me now. If you can slow him down again...."

Howard's eyes suddenly grew wide one second before he was flattened by Hunter's body slam. Howard's knife skittered across the floor. Hunter then turned to Ruth, a rage in his eyes like she had never seen, and pulled his own knife, a six-inch switchblade. He slashed at her and she jumped back. He slashed again and she backed away, but now she was backed into a wall. He came at her with a grin on his face.

"I'm gonna have fun slicing you up alive, like one of these goddam cows."

She saw the side of his face cave in before she heard the blast. Her own face was sprayed with blood, human blood. Hunter still stood there for a second, as if his massive body could go on without a brain, but then he slumped to the floor.

"That man would have killed you," the Greek said calmly, putting one hand out to steady her even as he held the smoking gun in the other.

"Thank you." Ruth was numb. "There's more of those guys waiting outside. I have to get Sheila and get out of here."

"I had your truck moved to the loading dock. Sheila's already hiding in it. Go out the employee entrance."

"You're a good man, Mr. Leonides."

Chapter 36

Upon hearing the shot, the security guards outside broke into a run for the processing building. The Genesis Riders were not far behind, including the one with his hands still handcuffed behind his back. By the time they got to the scene, the Greek had already stopped all the lines, roped off the scene, downloaded all the security footage and called the sheriff. Everyone knew that Sheriff Weakins had probably been told to keep his officers away from United Processing that day, but they'd have to come in response to a call reporting a fatal shooting. The Genesis Riders turned away at the sight of their leader's body and began running out of the plant, ignoring the security guards' orders to stay.

Ruth knew the Riders would soon be after her. Sheila's husband's house was twenty miles away and toward the west, away from the safety of Cosgrove County, but at least the road was straight and virtually empty, and she was averaging over ninety in the truck. She had had a short, loud argument with the Greek before she left over who should keep the gun. She won.

The plan had been for them to snatch Sheila's son, Bobby, from the playground of a nearby elementary school. Sheila had tried to persuade Ann, wife number one, to take both their children there for a picnic. They had picnicked there before, but Ann had been noncommittal when Sheila left the house in the morning. As kind and accommodating as Ann usually was, she didn't want to play the role of babysitter for her husband's second wife. Thus, they wasted ten miles and fifteen minutes detouring to the playground of the elementary school, which was empty when they pulled up.

When Sheila had first been taken as his second wife, her new husband, Paul, had moved them out of the tiny town where they had lived. He said he was no longer happy with his small, three-bedroom, air-conditioned house. His growing family needed more privacy, he insisted, more room to practice religion as the Lord and Reverend Ezekial ordained. And so Paul had moved his growing family back to his own family's old farmhouse. The wives both hated it. Sheila was put to work scraping and painting while wife number one was in charge of decorating. They were also required to set up an extra room for the expected wife number three. The house was hot, dusty and dirty, and half the windows wouldn't open, but Paul insisted they would have it fixed up in no time. Sheila's pay from the processing plant was funding the renovations. Sheila hated working in the house under Ann's supervision, but she had to be nice to her because Ann was in complete control of little Bobby, including during the entire day when Sheila was away working.

"See that blue farmhouse about a half mile ahead, set on that little rise? That's it, home sweet home. Let's go." Ruth could hear the determination in Sheila's voice.

"Hand me that burner phone in the glove compartment," Ruth ordered. She punched in Damien's number. The last she'd heard, Renee had been taken from Bible Land but had not been seen since.

"Um, good news," Damien answered. "Your sister's on her way to Cosgrove County right now."

"Oh thank you, thank you! Don's got her?"

"No, that plan didn't work. Dirk, the guy I live with, is taking her."

"But he's a Rider!"

"He's a good guy. Trust me. Your Dad's at the record store now, charging the batteries for his cycle."

"Where are you, Damien?"

"I'm at my father's house. The Riders might be after me. My father is here, talking to the security firm he hired to watch the plant. They told him the whole story. Hunter is dead. The Riders said you killed him. They all went off after you."

"Do they know I have Sheila?"

"They know you took somebody with you. But nobody can figure out her real name, or where she lives. The manifest has disappeared. They went off in all directions."

"Did they say anything about the boning room manager, the guy they call the Greek?"

"Didn't hear anything about that."

*** ***

At three in the afternoon, Stacey got the call back from Washington, D.C. she was waiting for. Golsch's voice was damped down as if he were taking her call during a meeting, and he was blunt.

"What do you want, Stacey?"

"We found the name and address of the woman you saw in the Penance video. We found the names and addresses of the women they punished like that in the past. We have all their records. We have enough evidence to charge 47 men with kidnapping and rape of 106 women."

"I'm in D.C."

"You have to speak to the governor. I can't get through to her."

"I told you I'm in D.C."

"They're taking my friend right now to that torture chamber you saw on that video."

She heard him sigh. It was a nice, human, concerned sigh. "What do you want me to do?"

"Use your fucking phone. Tell her there's going to be another video soon. Tell her I'll make sure it gets online even if I have to put it on the legislature's website. Tell her everyone will know she had the chance to stop this brutality – but refused to."

"I believe you might actually do that, Stacey." She thought he heard a smile in his voice.

"That's what Roland would have done."

There was a pause on the line, then Golsch's voice suddenly crackled with energy. He wasn't speaking to Stacey. "Clear the room. This meeting is over. Benjamin, get me Governor Adams on the line. Tell her it's an emergency."

*** ***

Sheila's owner, Paul, was a small, dapper man with greying hair and gold-rimmed glasses. He obviously had heard the truck pull up and the tromping of Sheila and Ruth's shoes on the wooden front porch. He opened the door before they even reached it.

"Naomi." He used Sheila's concubine name. "Now, I told you to use the back door except when we are entering or exiting the house as a family." Then he noticed Ruth coming in behind her. "And I definitely did not give permission for you to make an acquaintance outside of the home."

Sheila was every bit as tall as he was. "I've come to get my son."

He didn't pick up on her tone, or notice her stance. "Has Ann asked you to bring him somewhere?"

"Ann has nothing to do with it."

He was slowly catching on. "Making light of my rules is dangerous, Naomi. God has ordained your place in this household, and your obedience. I'm telling you seriously, Naomi, you should think twice before you flout God's rule."

Ruth stepped around Sheila, pulled her gun and put the barrel to his chest. "There's a new God in town."

She made him drop his pants, and Sheila tightened his belt around his ankles. Then Sheila went back to the truck for rope, and they tied his feet together and his hands to the stair rails. They searched him and took away his phone. All the while they keep an ear out for Ann. There was no telling whose side Ann would take. It was certain she didn't have a phone of her own. Ruth followed Sheila down the dark hallway to the back of the house, where the women and children were kept. They found Ann half asleep in a chair while her own six-year-old daughter and Sheila's son Bobby played alongside each other.

"Bobby, come on." Sheila's decisive command got Bobby moving.

"What are you doing?" Ann was still only half awake.

"Come with us." Ruth commanded. She felt a little drunk with the power the gun gave her. They rushed Ann and her daughter out, jamming everyone into the truck. "You can leave with us," Ruth explained as they pulled away. "We're going to a place where women are free. Or you can stay here."

"He's my real husband. I'm his real wife."

"Suit yourself. I'll drop you off a mile down the road. You and your daughter can walk back and untie him. We'll be long gone by then."

Ruth drove a mile and a half before letting them off. There was always the danger that some friendly citizen would pick mother and daughter up and give them a ride home, but Ruth figured she'd just have to take that chance.

"Bye, Ann. Hope you get home all right." Sheila surprised everybody by saying that.

Ann, standing on the shoulder of the road, holding her daughter's hand, looked up, her face registering surprise. "Bye, Naomi, or whatever your name is. I didn't hate you. I hope you get free."

Ruth pulled away, quickly gaining speed. The truck was registered in Damien's name so the state police, the county sheriff's office and Conception Control would have no interest in tracking it. To make sure she couldn't be tracked, she had turned off all mapping apps. She had simply memorized the route from the plant to Sheila's house and from there to Cosgrove. The disadvantage was she now had to take the most obvious route.

If the Genesis Riders knew Sheila's address, they'd be waiting for her somewhere along that route. Fortunately, Sheila had stolen and destroyed the manifest from the contract workers' van as she exited it at the plant that morning. The addresses of the captive women were kept so secret that it might take some time for the Riders to figure out where she lived. Ruth's plan was simply to step on the gas and hope for the best.

It was about forty miles from Ruth's house to the Cosgrove County line. Since the Riders were no respecters of county lines, she figured she'd have to make it about fifty miles, to within ten miles of Cosgrove City itself, before they would be safe. They were about halfway there, speeding through flat fields of browning sorghum, just past a deserted intersection, when she saw the bright flash of the sun reflecting off a motorcycle coming her way.

Two motorcycles. Three. Two of them stopped and formed a roadblock. The other kept speeding towards her. From this distance, they couldn't know for sure it was her. They must be stopping every truck, she guessed. She yelled for Sheila and Bobby to get down on the floor as she stopped. She checked her nine-millimeter. But there was no way she would start a gunfight from the cab with the two of them on board.

She jumped out of the cab into the road, leaving the motor running, as the cycle approached. She took a wide stance, making sure her gun was visible in its holster. The Rider pulled to a stop next to her, blonde hair, pencil thin moustache, sweaty, anxious face. He wasn't showing a gun.

"Come with us, bitch, or you're as good as dead."

"You don't understand. I'd *rather* be dead." She turned and opened the cab door. "And I'll run over your friends if I have to."

She jumped back in the truck before he could react. But he followed her. And he did have a gun, a large chrome revolver that he now pulled from his saddlebag and pointed at her face. She pulled her own gun and pointed it at him. She heard the other two motorcycles revving. His eyes shifted back toward his friends. She suddenly revved the truck motor and put it in gear, backing toward the intersection fifty yards behind.

"Stay down!" she yelled at Sheila and Bobby. She wasn't used to backing this fast, and the truck was squirreling all over the road. The blonde Rider recovered his composure and easily caught up to her. Riding on the shoulder, keeping his distance from the swerving truck, he pulled his gun and shot. A tremendous blast echoed in the cab. She yelled for the other two to stay down. The truck sank down in front. He had shot a tire. The truck swerved backwards off the road right near the intersection and stopped. He took another shot, which bounced off the rim of the same tire with an ear-piercing twang. Stacey didn't dare start a gunfight. His bullets could cut through the cab like butter. The other two cyclists were getting close.

The blonde Rider took another shot, this time toward the back tire, and missed. Ruth calculated that, to escape, she'd have to kill all three of them, change a flat tire, and reach Cosgrove before any of the other Riders found out about it. Not to mention the sheriff's department which, she knew, would be helping the Riders in the search. Sheila and Bobby could be hurt in the crossfire. She had only two choices: to live as a captive or to die fighting. She jumped out of the truck, gun in hand, but pointing it down toward the ground.

She backed down the length of the truck, keeping an eye on the blonde Rider, who seemed to be following her, but at an almost leisurely pace. He seemed sure she was trapped, but not sure enough that he didn't train his gun on her. She could end it all by pointing her gun at him. He probably wouldn't shoot her, as he hadn't before, but chances were good that one of the other two Riders, who were almost upon them, would do her the favor of ending her life.

She was now twenty yards behind the truck, far enough so that no shots aimed at her would hit Sheila or Bobby in the cab. She heard sirens suddenly yelping close behind her, brakes screeching to a stop, doors opening and closing. She swore she would not be taken by the sheriff's men either. The two other Riders had also just arrived and were enjoying themselves shooting out the truck's back tire. Bobby started screaming from inside the truck. She heard a lot of yelling and commotion behind her. She knew she had only ten seconds to live. She decided to take a Rider with her.

A deafening barrage of gunfire behind her shook the ground. The smoke from the shots clouded her vision. Before she could even bring her gun up, all three Riders twitched, jerked and fell to the ground. Her first thought was she'd now have to hurry up and kill herself. But she hardly had raised her gun an inch when it was knocked out of her hand and she was grabbed from behind by impossibly strong arms.

"Let me go. Or shoot me. I don't care."

"State police, Ma'am. It's over. We're freeing all the women."

Chapter 37

There were only four people allowed in the meeting: Stacey, Martha, Robert Golsch and Heinrich Heine, Speaker of the House of Representatives and head of the Certainty Party.

"Let's put this meeting in context." Stacey couldn't help but smiling. "Reverend Ezekial has been arrested and charged with 78 counts of kidnapping, and trafficking, fourteen counts of rape, and numerous counts of assault, not to mention the failure to pay the minimum wage. Warrants have been issued for the arrest of 41 men who kidnapped, bought, sold, had sexual intercourse with, engaged in corporal punishment of, or failed to pay the minimum wage to hundreds of women. Investigations are continuing to learn the names of all those who aided or abetted in this scheme. Recall proceedings are being brought against Sheriff Weakins of Neola County."

"The women?" Martha asked.

"They have already located and freed 56 of them, and they know the whereabouts of most of the others and are actively searching them out.

"You've lost all your support," Stacey now turned to Heine. "Your main inspirational leader, Reverend Ezekial, will be going to jail, probably for the rest of his life. Your supposedly biblical laws have been exposed as perverted desires of sick men. We're here to convince you to change course."

"We still have a majority of the legislature, Ms. Davenporn, and we'll continue to have it for the next two years. Even after that, we will probably still control it, as 82% of incumbents are reelected on average in this state."

"Twenty-six of your members in the House have been indicted. And the state police haven't even started looking in any other counties outside of Neola."

"And Golsch Industries is through with you guys," Robert Golsch added. "What you did was depraved. And then you disguised it with this biblical bullshit."

"Why are we here? Why are we even talking to the Certainty Party?" Martha's scowl said more than her words did.

"We're here," Stacey put her hand on Martha's arm, "to put Kansas back on its historical, moderate path. We're here to persuade Speaker Heine that all of these Ezekial-inspired laws, Feto-Terrorism, Conception Control, Reform of the Professions, are out of the mainstream of Kansans' thought, and they ought to be repealed."

"You think a couple of indictments can change the whole course of this thing?" Heine scoffed.

"Forty-one indictments and more to come, unless the Certainty Party immediately repeals all of these laws."

"We still control the legislature. We still make all the laws." Heine's arrogance seemed to be receding, but he still clung to the mathematics.

Stacey held his gaze and spoke very slowly. "The police haven't finished yet. And we have the book, the book the police are working from. They got the book from us, Speaker Heine. The book shows you bought a concubine yourself. The book shows you're keeping her in the basement."

Heine was struck silent. His face blanched. "What do you want?" he croaked.

Heine first tried holding out for immunity for all the men involved. Then, backing off somewhat, he asked for immunity for all the men who had not yet committed any violence against the women. Stacey guessed he had not "consummated" his relationship with his concubine yet. When Stacey said she would consider that, Martha stomped out of the room, ending the meeting.

Stacey caught up with her in their office suite.

"Please, Martha, I won't do this without your consent. But I think what he's offering might be the best deal we can get." Martha finally turned to meet her gaze. "And even if some of the men aren't criminally prosecuted, the women can still sue them in civil court. The women will sue, and they will win. The only thing Heine is holding out for now is that the men, the non-violent men who haven't touched the women, will not be criminally prosecuted. And, in return, all those horrible laws that treat women like cattle will be immediately repealed."

"It's not right to just forgive all those crimes."

"I admit it, Martha. It's not right. But CP still has control of the legislature. Conception Control and Feto-Terrorism and Reform of the Professions are still on the books. Real people will be hurt by those laws if we don't make a deal."

Martha's influence had grown over the course of the session. She was now considered the conscience of the Independents, the group that had finally forestalled the worst proposals of the Certainty Party. Stacey wouldn't do any deal unless Martha agreed. She asked Martha to think about it overnight.

The next morning, Martha trudged into Stacey's office, looking like she hadn't slept at all.

"I trust you, Stacey," she began. "I haven't felt that way about anybody since … well, since Roland. You are a worthy successor to Roland, and I don't mean any kind of irony by that. I hate to see any of those guys not criminally prosecuted, but if you think this is the best deal we can get, I'll go along with it. And the Independents will, too."

"Thanks, Martha." That wasn't enough to say. Stacey knew she would spend the rest of her own life in politics – which, for her, meant living her life for others. She was getting used to the feeling of being needed in that way, used to knowing that no one else could do the job as well as she could. It was her calling. But it was also just a job. She'd always hoped for just a little bit more from life than just a job. She had brushed off, ignored, compromised, even hurt quite a few people to accomplish what she needed to in this job. She sometimes wondered if it was worth it.

"I'm really proud to be your friend, Martha. It means a lot to me."

Martha still looked skeptical. Stacey's heart sank. But if she had learned one good habit from politics, it was never to give up.

"Really, it means a lot to me. You don't understand. You're the first female friend I ever really had."

"No."

"Yes. I've been thinking about it. It's really true. I loved my Daddy. Then I loved my drugs. Then I loved my career. And I loved a couple of men. But women? They were just obstacles in my way. Until you came along. I mean it. I really hope we stay friends."

* * *   * * *

Grant arrived in Kansas the following Sunday. Stacey met him at the airport, clasping her tiny pocketbook in both hands at her waist because she wasn't sure if a hug or a kiss was appropriate. Grant's look was just as tentative. They hesitated for a second before the baggage carousel, then just shook hands. "You're looking great. Starting to show a little bit," he ventured.

"Thanks. I do have time to wash and comb my hair now that that crazy election is over."

They were both nervous about what to do next, and they ended up sitting at a tiny table in the airport restaurant. They both said they weren't hungry, but then they both ordered food. Grant excused himself and then came back a few minutes later with a double shot of bourbon he'd bought at the bar. He poured it into his soda and took a long drink.

"A double shot? I didn't think I was *that* scary," she tried to joke. He smiled.

"You really are a force of nature. I can't believe all that you've accomplished."

"It wasn't me this time. They risked their lives, Ruth and Amy, Damien and my Dad."

"You've got to tell me all the details." He took a gulp of his drink. "I wish I could have helped."

"I don't think the action hero kind of thing is for you. Remember …."

"Ha ha," he cut her off. There had been a time last summer during her election campaign when he had regularly carried a gun. The townspeople had made fun of his awkward way with it. Then, when real danger had faced Stacey, he had tried to protect her, succeeding only in shooting himself in the hip.

He was still sensitive about that incident. But he comforted himself with the idea that she still liked him. He took another sip and sat there appreciating how much fun it was to once again be the object of her attention. But he snapped out of his reverie. "There must be something I can do."

"Yes, maybe," she answered. "There might be something you could still do. As a lawyer, I mean. The Greek's been charged with murder in Neola County. There are three eyewitnesses who will testify for the defense. No prosecution witnesses. He can't possibly be convicted – in any place but in Neola County. We need to get the trial moved to another county."

"I'll do anything you want, Stacey. But it's not my area of expertise, and I'm not even sure what are the grounds for moving a trial out of a county. Maybe …."

She cut him off. "There's only one judge in Neola County. He was arrested last night for keeping two local women as concubines in his basement. He bought them directly from the Genesis Riders. I don't think it'll take too much expertise to make the argument the case should be moved." She smiled.

"Are you up for it, Grant?'"

*** ***

The deal with the Certainty Party was done, the legislature was in hiatus, the Greek's trial had been moved to Cosgrove County. Stacey and Grant were relaxing at her apartment, slouched at opposite ends of the sofa. He took the opportunity to tell her the very latest news from Boston.

Eleni had finally sued Grant himself. In the lawsuit, she claimed that Grant had withheld the Recognition of Diluted References form from her and, had she been fully informed of the possibility that his reference would mean less because he was in love with her, she would never have allowed herself to be induced into having an affair with him. Amos then fired Grant as soon as Eleni's suit against him was filed. He told Grant it was nothing personal, but he had to protect the company. The Massachusetts bar had begun an inquest into Grant's behavior with Eleni and, "in the interest of public safety," suspended his privilege to practice law until the investigation was complete.

"What's going to happen to me?" he griped now to Stacey. He seemed more angry than worried. "What can I do now? Do you think they'd let me practice law here in Kansas?"

"I'll give you a good reference," she smiled. "I'll say they might as well let you practice law, as you're not good for much of anything else – certainly no good with a gun."

"Okay," he laughed, "so I'm not very good with the gun thing. But maybe now people won't need to carry guns all the time, not in the new Kansas, the kinder, gentler Kansas, that you created."

She felt her anger rise. "I didn't *create* this Kansas! It's always been here. People here are nice. I've told you that a thousand times. But sometimes people just go off the deep end. It happens. I've done it myself."

"Yes, you have."

In the dead silence that followed his remark, she stared at him, mouth slack, eyes wide. She realized she valued his opinion about what kind of person she was. She knew she could go on without him, but she didn't think it would be any fun.

She studied his expression when he didn't say anything more. He obviously knew all her past history. He had watched as her character flaws were magnified by the media coverage of her campaign. He had personally felt the brunt of some of her bad decisions. And he was still here. What did it mean?

Stacey thought she might as well get to the point. "So, I've gone off the deep end, a lot. Do you love me anyway?"

He smiled to himself, shook his head, broke eye contact. He stared at the wall as if there were writing on it that he was trying to read. "What can I say? You're still my hero." He read a little further. "That's a yes."